I ONLY HAUNT TO BE WITH YOU

ELLEN RIGGS

Free Prequel

Rescuing this sassy dachshund would be a lot easier if he were actually alive.

Novice psychic Janelle Brighton has been framed for murder and a cocky canine ghost holds the key to the mystery. Can they rescue each other before a killer prevails? Join Ellen Riggs' author newsletter at **ellenriggs.com/mystic-mutts-opt-in** to get this FREE prequel to the Mystic Mutts Mysteries series.

I Only Haunt to Be With You

Copyright © 2022 Ellen Riggs

ISBN 978-1-990613-02-9 eBook
ISBN 978-1-990613-03-6 Book
ISBN 978-1-990613-66-1 AudioBook
ASIN B09KSD2NSB Kindle
ASIN 1990613039 Paperback

Publisher: Ellen Riggs
www.ellenriggs.com
Cover designer: Lou Harper
Editor: Serena Clarke
2405051627

CHAPTER ONE

The sun was rising over Main Street on a frosty late November day when Renata Scott came through the door of Whimsy, my jewelry and gift store, carrying a plate. A charmed doorbell gave the spritely jingle that always announced my best friend's arrival.

Each day, Ren baked and delivered something new to taste test. Each day, I pronounced the sample utterly delectable. And each day I reminded myself how lucky we were to have reconnected after parting over a traumatic incident in high school. It was a bonus that she was so talented in the kitchen and I had no doubt her new venture, Flour Girl Bakery, would be a huge hit when she formally launched next week.

"No doubt at all?" My black-and-tan dachshund trotted over to greet Ren with his typical salty commentary. "It never pays to be overconfident, Janelle. Unless you're me."

"Morning, folks," Ren called, making sure Bijou, her fluffy apricot poodle mix, was safely inside before nudging the door closed with her knee and locking it. My store wouldn't be open to the public for hours but I liked to arrive early to enjoy the peace and hang out with my friends.

Whimsy was sandwiched between two stores on a property Ren

and I had bought with a lot of help and a dangerously sneaky strategy. Flour Girl Bakery sat on one side. The other store was still vacant because my nemesis, Main Street megalomaniac Oscar Knight, was blackballing us in the community. We were content to wait for exactly the right fit since our little strip was a labor of love.

My other close friend, Sinda Joffrey, came up from the basement when she heard Ren's footsteps. Despite being in her seventies, Sinda often beat me to the store, eager to get started on creating jewelry in her workshop downstairs.

"Smells like cinnamon," Sinda said. "What's on the menu, Ren?"

"Pumpkin cheesecake squares." Ren's radiant smile and big black eyes made her stunning despite a hairnet and splattered apron. "How does that sound for breakfast?"

"Wonderful. Beats oatmeal." When we'd met in Gran's retirement community, Sinda could have passed for a typical senior citizen. She was far from typical, as I'd discovered. "I feel younger by the day thanks in part to your baking."

Ren found space on the counter for the plate. "The secret's in the butter. Does the heart good, no matter what the experts say."

"Live hard and die young," Bixby said. "Then do it all again. At least, that worked for me."

We laughed and he puffed out his chest. My sassy canine sidekick was full of himself, but he also had the rich and buttery heart of a hero.

"Hit me with a double, Ren," I said, as she divvied up the squares. "We need to build capacity for the holiday."

In less than a week, we'd celebrate Thanksgiving together at the Brighton manor. The old house belonged to my mom, who was still down south visiting my grandmother. I was thankful to be on better terms with Mom and equally thankful she was away. Adding to the heap of gratitude, I was thankful Gran's cousin Liberty was down there with them. She was helping Mom get to the bottom of a mysterious magical threat in what was supposed to be a safe gated community.

"Liberty is a treat best enjoyed from afar," said Mr. Bixby. "An acquired taste I have yet to acquire. Same goes for your boyfriends. I prefer to be the only guy in our crowd."

Police Chief Andrew Gillock wasn't my boyfriend, although I quite liked the idea. So much so that the large vase of sunflowers he gave me when the store launched still sat on a shelf in the back room. Their heavy heads had drooped but they continued to inspire me.

"Inspire false hope, you mean," Bixby said. "Opposites may attract but they don't endure. Look only as far as the tragic romance stories everyone hates to love."

"Lighten up, wiener boy," Bijou said, prancing past him. "Let Witchy and Renny-ren-ren have their dreams. Anything could happen."

My dachshund gave Bijou a couple of quick jabs with his long nose. These dogs were incredibly unique, with their magical gifts and sassy chatter, but they were still dogs. Bixby was the first ghost canine I'd helped transition back to life and in his mind that made him the resident alpha. But Bijou had haunted my store for decades before crossing back to join Renata, which gave her a strong claim on the place. That led to posturing and verbal slings, mostly intended to entertain us and each other. The sassy duo brought delight every day and when the need arose, they saved our lives.

It was a good arrangement, except for the part about saving our lives. It happened more often than it should, even in Wyldwood Springs. My hometown was arguably the prettiest place in all of hill country, with its many spring-fed streams, quaint bridges and well-maintained parks. Beneath the beauty, however, was a decided dash of menace. When I left the Brighton manor every morning, I was never quite sure I'd make it home.

"Woe is you," Mr. Bixby said, strolling back to me across gleaming oak floors. "Sounds a little melodramatic."

In this case, it didn't "sound" like anything at all. My vague fears had been nothing more than silent musings, but Bixby never allowed privacy to hold him back from monitoring my thoughts. As someone with moderate psychic abilities, I found it ironic that I'd ended up rescuing a dog that could pass in and out of my own mind at will.

"Not just any dog, Janelle." He stared up at me as I polished jewelry with a special shammy. Sinda's pieces already glittered in the sunlight pouring through the wide front windows, but I tended to them like children. "I'm a very special dog who deserves at least as much attention as you give those baubles."

"You don't appreciate affection," I said, aloud. "I do try."

He made a sweeping gesture with his nose. It was a command to set him on the counter, which I promptly obeyed. "I like it on my own terms. That's the only thing I have in common with a cat."

"Aside from an imperious manner," Sinda said, scratching his ears fondly. "Some might even say snooty."

He leaned into her fingers. "It comes with my pedigree and I wouldn't change a thing. I try to keep my nose high and my confidence higher. You ladies"—he peered over the edge of the counter at Bijou—"and the poodle, would do well to follow my example."

"He's not wrong," Ren said, handing me a paper plate and a fork. "I'm so anxious I barely sleep at night."

"You need a lava lamp," Bixby said. "Knocks Janelle right out. I wonder if it's been charmed, like the doorbell."

Taking my first bite of fall on a fork, I smiled. "Possibly. I've had it since I was a kid and I wouldn't put it past Mom to sedate me with spells."

"Can hardly blame her," he said. "You were a little firebrand."

"I wasn't *that* bad. Besides, she should have been able to stay ahead of me. I'm only half the psychic she is."

"Nonsense," Mr. Bixby said. "I poked around her mind a good bit before she left. You're different, that's all. And you most certainly have a spark of originality you didn't get from her."

That part was true. Just before my teenage hormones kicked in, I developed the power to stun people with a minor shock. My inability to control either my temper or that power had eventually resulted in a prom night fiasco that put me on a collision course with Oscar Knight and his vile son. I left Wyldwood Springs and built a successful career during a wild ride through the best resorts in the country. Two months ago, I came home to face my past, rebuild relationships with Mom and Ren, and... well, start over. Best decision I ever made. And also the worst, since Oscar was still gunning for me. My powers were growing, but they got away on me sometimes. I'd had success in putting some killers out of commission by frying their mental circuitry, raising plenty of questions with Chief Gillock. I'd also bungled some spells rather spectacularly and burned what was meant to flourish. In short, it was hit and miss, and because my dubious gifts fell outside the normal parameters for magical kind, I didn't have much guidance.

Sometimes I missed my old life on the run, but the one gift I valued above all others was my ability to bring ghost dogs back to life. It had started with Bixby, continued with Bijou, and then, most recently, Harold, an Australian shepherd who belonged to Cousin Liberty.

"Must we talk about Hairball?" Mr. Bixby said, aloud.

Sinda laughed. "You weren't talking about anything. How about cutting us in on the conversation?"

"Sorry," I said. "My ability to switch channels with Bixby is becoming so automatic I'm not always aware of it. I know it's rude."

The dog stretched out on the counter and Ren moved the plate of cheesecake out of the way. We weren't overly fussy about paw prints and dog hair but her customers certainly would be. It was a good thing the universe had sent her a non-shedding, perky dog that people wouldn't complain about. Bijou had chosen Renata and they were the perfect match.

Mr. Bixby snorted and then rolled onto his side in a warm beam of sunlight. With winter on the horizon, I'd need to pick up more cute coats for him. I already had a snazzy blue bomber.

His snort turned into a grumble. "How can I possibly catch a chill when you rarely let my paws touch pavement?"

"Maybe I will when people stop trying to kill us," I said. "I wonder if I could make you a magic-proof parka? Like the coyote-proof ones with spikes."

Now he groaned. "I don't like my chances of coming out of that spell alive."

Ren layered on a heavy sigh. Our efforts at learning magic had been spotty, at best. We usually got where we needed to go but not without some drama during the drive.

"We're doing better," she told him. "Our last session went well. No injuries or fatalities."

He rolled his visible eye at her. "Hardly worth bragging about."

"Gotta start somewhere," I said. "With our businesses gearing up, it's not like we have a ton of spare time."

"Time won't be your only problem if you don't hone your chops," he said. "I doubt Oscar Knight is going to cut you a break when you keep stepping on his toes."

"Seems like you get all the credit when things go well and I get all the blame when they tank."

He offered a deep and melodious chuckle. "Sounds about right. We're the perfect team."

Actually, we were. When he wasn't talking smack—and even when he was—this dog had my back. He'd helped me avoid the machinations of several miscreants, magical or otherwise. Furthermore, he'd recently stopped Cousin Liberty from killing me by accident. At the time, she'd been trapped by a powerful curse from Oscar Knight. With help from my friends, I'd been able to transfuse her with my own power and bring her back from a state worse than death. However, I hadn't felt the same since.

Mr. Bixby sat up and stared at me. "How so? And why am I just hearing about it now?"

"What?" Ren said. "I missed a few beats there."

Sinda and Ren could hear the conversation when Mr. Bixby and I spoke aloud but much of our dialogue transpired in silence. It was safer that way. Babbling to him in my early days home had gained me a reputation for eccentricity. Then Liberty resurfaced to steal the spotlight.

"Liberty does take the cheesecake for weirdness," Bixby said, leaning over to sniff the baked goods.

I moved the plate away. "You can have the crumbs when we're done."

"I am not a dog for crumbs, in case you hadn't noticed."

"Let him have a piece if you like," Ren said. "Bijou got the first bite. She has the most refined nose and palate. She can tell when my measurements are off by the slightest smidge."

Bixby peered over the edge of the counter at Bijou. "A good sniffer is worth something."

It was rare for him to offer a morsel of praise to Bijou, but they'd formed a united front against Harold. The Aussie had retained a flair for wind when he came over, and nearly blew the smaller dogs to smithereens sometimes. I told myself it was accidental, but with Liberty as his leader, Harold couldn't help but be quirky, too.

"Which brings us back around to what happened with Liberty," Mr. Bixby said. "Tell us how you haven't been the same."

I took another bite of the cheesecake and shrugged. "I can't explain it."

"Try. What you don't share could get us all killed."

I patted my lips with a napkin. "It's not like that. I just have this vague sense of... I don't know... doom. Probably just a vibe left over from Liberty's incarceration."

"So she stole all your magical gifts and left you with doom? Nothing else?"

I tried to wrap words around the sensation inside. "It's like someone came into my house and rearranged everything. You know I like to be organized but Liberty is cavalier. When she visited my mental space she flung things around, and I'm still looking for them."

Bixby was on his paws now, muzzle raised as if to sniff out any evasion in my words. "Is anything missing?"

I shrugged. "I don't think so. It's more like she left things behind."

"Other than a sense of doom?" Ren asked. "What a terrible hostess gift."

"Right? Especially when I was always such an optimist."

My dog grunted. "You lived your life on the run from magical criminals. There was precious little room for optimism."

"But I always escaped, and still do. Plus, with a new mission of rescuing ghost dogs I have the best reason for optimism."

I touched the pendant dangling from my neck. It was a small gold dachshund with ears flying and an emerald chip for an eye. As always, it warmed my fingertips, as much if not more than the real thing. Ren did the same with the little poodle pendant around her neck. That made Sinda smile. For many years, she'd created these pieces from visions of dogs that appeared in her imagination. She'd suspected they were ghosts but had no idea she'd meet someone capable of bringing them back for a second inning.

"Dear friend, I'm worried about you," she said, touching my arm and pouring cool, calming energy into me. "It sounds like your cousin left you with a mess. She did suggest there might be fallout from your energy transfer, as I recall."

I nodded. "I'll speak to Liberty about it. For the moment, I just worry about being able to find my magical tools when I need them."

Ren's perfectly groomed eyebrows gathered. "Hopefully we'll

have some time in the clear. Liberty seems like a good match for Oscar."

"He took her down before," I said. "Albeit with help from half a dozen cronies. But what's to stop him from doing it again? She said the Knights have had a long feud with the Brightons."

"And then Liberty sprung the story on Oscar's wife," Mr. Bixby said. "You'd think he'd have divulged the story first."

I continued to pat the dog and hold my pendant. It gave me a sense of stability. "Mrs. Knight was so nice. I don't understand why she's with a snake like him."

The word wasn't a random choice. Whenever Oscar got near me, snakes seemed to fill my very soul. Now I knew why: it was Brightons versus Knights, and had been for generations.

"Is that the sense of doom you were talking about?" Mr. Bixby said. "Liberty had some nerve destroying your rainbows." He looked at Ren. "Isn't that what you saw in Janelle's aura? Rainbows?"

Ren's smile emerged from behind a cloud. "Actually, yeah. And it's still there, in case you're wondering, Janny."

I laughed. "That's reassuring. And I love that you can see them again."

"Only when I'm calm and focused, which is pretty rare these days."

"That's the challenge," I said. "When I asked Mom how to stay focused she was so dismissive. Apparently, you just do."

I circled back to being thankful Mom was away with Liberty. For the moment, I'd enjoy every single moment of my time alone.

"You're never alone with a pedigreed dachshund in your head," Mr. Bixby said. "Not to mention a stranger staring in the window. Who have we here?"

Outside, a woman with wispy gray hair was standing with her nose pressed to the glass. And she looked utterly petrified.

CHAPTER TWO

I probably would have been more worried if the woman hadn't been holding a plastic tub of muffins. Given all my friends and I had been through together, we could probably handle a woman offering what appeared to be bran bombs.

"Don't get cocky," Mr. Bixby said, as I scooped him up and carried him to the door. "You know what that cleansing spell did to the pipes at home. Too much bran is a bad idea, especially from unknown sources."

"Right, right, right," Bijou said, trotting along beside me. "No more toxins for Renata."

We had been well and thoroughly poisoned by people showing up here bearing gifts that looked more appealing than bran muffins, and the poodle had done her best, even in ghost form, to keep Ren from partaking.

"What doesn't kill you makes you stronger," I said, glancing at my entourage. "Agreed?"

Sinda patted her abdomen. "I feel pretty good but at my age you don't mess with the inner workings without regret."

I unlocked the door and opened it with a friendly smile. "Good morning. What can I do for you today?"

The woman's eyes were still wide and her breath unusually ragged for Main Street on a regular morning. "Are you Janelle Brighton?"

Nodding, I stepped back to allow her inside. "Welcome to Whimsy."

She passed in front of me, keeping as much distance between us as she could. Perhaps she was just nervous about the dogs, who were both blatantly sniffing her.

"Clear," Mr. Bixby said.

"Clear," Bijou echoed.

This was new and I assumed they were telling me the stranger didn't reek of what Mr. Bixby commonly called magical flatulence. To the dogs, people like Oscar Knight apparently smelled like a mixture of sulfur, rotten yard waste and roasting roadkill. Just the thought of it was enough to put me off the muffins.

"Pass on the muffins," Bijou confirmed. "Hydrogenated fats. We're butter people."

The woman pulled a stack of napkins out of her apron pocket and offered them to us. Then she dangled the plastic tub in our direction and nodded encouragingly. Each of us selected a muffin, lining them up on the counter, like grenades that needed to be monitored.

Ren introduced Sinda and then herself. "My bakery next door opens in a week."

"I'm Valerie Fairchild," the woman said. "The new owner of the Beanstalk Café."

Mine wasn't the only gasp; it wasn't even the loudest. "The Beanstalk Café is reopening? Already?"

Valerie nodded. "I know it's a shock. It surprised me, too, when Mr. Knight called and offered it to me. I'd been on his list for retail space for nearly a decade but couldn't get my foot in the door."

Mr. Bixby chuckled. "Because someone had to be carted out feet first before it could happen. Mitzy Lennox is barely cold."

I started to set him on the counter, but changed my mind. Valerie might be offended to see a dog so close to her baked goods. Instead, I gave Bixby the standard squeeze to keep his voice down. Not that she could understand him. And not that it would work. All it did was help me feel calmer in a strange situation.

"Congratulations, Valerie," I said. "We know better than most people how hard it is to get a foothold on Main Street." Gesturing to my friends, I added, "We got very lucky."

"If you call nearly getting killed lucky," Mr. Bixby said. "Having spent some decades dead, I do not."

She set her muffin container on one of my empty display tables. Later, when the store opened, the table would hold some of Sinda's designs. We kept the jewels locked away overnight to deter break-ins. Most of her pieces were very affordable and only had semi-precious stones. The true value came in their originality, and more importantly, the bit of magic she inadvertently added. We'd sold a few dozen pieces and already people were coming back for more, claiming their pendant, ring or earrings had brought good fortune in the form of a new job, a new boyfriend or even a cash windfall. It wasn't something Sinda did deliberately, but her creativity came from a core of goodness and was baked into the mix, like Ren's addictive treats.

"I thought I'd die before my dream of owning a café came true," Valerie said. "But I guess after what happened to Mitzy Lennox, no one else on the list was willing to take a chance on the Beanstalk."

Ren, Sinda and I exchanged a look. What happened to Mitzy on the premises of the café she'd run for decades would be enough to scare most people away. Valerie Fairchild must be braver than she had seemed. In fact, her breathing had slowed almost to normal.

"You must have just opened," Ren said. "I walked past a couple of days ago and wondered what would happen to the place. I worked at the Beanstalk for years, you know."

"So I heard," Valerie said. "My aunt lived in Wyldwood all her life and I worked as a project manager in Chicago. Always wanted to come back but didn't make it till after she passed, unfortunately. I don't know what she'd say about the circumstances."

Sinda reached out and touched Valerie's arm, no doubt delivering a hit of courage. "She'd say it's time to make the best of it, I'm sure. Some opportunities come wrapped in brown paper packaging."

"With big black bows," Mr. Bixby added.

"I'll spruce the place up a little," Valerie said. "And change the signage when I come up with a new name. For now, there's only a few things on offer but I'll expand gradually."

"That sounds like a great plan," I said. "We're starting small, too."

Her eyes dropped to the floor and she mumbled, "There's just one problem, and I hoped you could help, Janelle."

"Me? How?"

When her eyes rose again to meet mine, they shone with tears. "The café is haunted."

"What makes you say so? I've been in and out of the Beanstalk since I was a kid and never saw anything strange." Glancing at Ren, I asked, "You?"

Renata shook her head. "I was usually there on my own before the sun came up and it was always peaceful."

"Maybe your imagination is acting up," Sinda said, giving Valerie's arm another squeeze. "After what happened there, it would be understandable."

"I know what I heard," Valerie said. "Clicking. Clunking. Heavy breathing. A cold breeze passed through me a few times last evening while I was cleaning. What if it's Mitzy? She never wanted to give the place up."

The rest of us stared at each other in consternation. Mitzy definitely hadn't wanted to go. Had she found a way to stick around? Take her revenge on Oscar by driving out successors?

Valerie swept her arm around. "Your store had a reputation for being haunted, Janelle. I wondered what you'd done about it."

I glanced down at Bijou, now leaning against Ren's shins and gazing up at her adoringly. Whimsy had been haunted by the poodle for decades before I pulled her back. Subsequently, we had a temporary ghostly visitor in the form of Harold, Cousin Liberty's dog. Currently, we were ghost-free and I hoped it might stay that way till I got my sea legs in business.

"There were plenty of rumors about this store being haunted," I said. "There are always stories like that in Wyldwood. You can see it's quiet and serene now."

"Thank goodness," Mr. Bixby said. "Most ghosts are disruptive. I was a model of decorum compared to the others we've met."

Sinda gave the dachshund in my arms a wink. While she hadn't been able to see or hear Mr. Bixby when he inhabited her store down south, they'd been constant companions nonetheless and he'd given her comfort when her husband passed. Now she enjoyed chatting with him and he spent a fair bit of time in her workshop downstairs.

Not all ghosts were so restrained, especially if the specter happened to be human. Our family ghost, Sir Nigel Boswell, had been a major disruption during my upbringing, and while I'd grown to value our butler, I wasn't sorry he'd gone down south with Mom. In my limited experience, even the most benevolent ghost could be demanding.

And I'd only met benevolent ghosts.

If Mitzy Lennox was back and planning to maintain a hold on her store, I didn't like Valerie's chances of getting the fresh start she craved. Mitzy wasn't benevolent in life and she'd met a shocking end at the hands of a criminal. I doubted she'd come back with a warm welcome for the new owner.

Valerie Fairchild gave a heavy sigh. "I hoped you could help,

Janelle. There are challenges enough without a ghost chasing customers out."

Mr. Bixby stirred under my arm. "What does she think you are? A ghostbuster?"

I'd helped three ghost dogs cross back over, and lived with Sir Nigel. Perhaps the term wasn't as ridiculous as Bixby made it sound.

"Then put it on a business card and start making some extra coin," he said. "*Not*. I was joking."

Patting his head, I reassured him silently that I had no intention of applying my unique gifts more broadly. In fact, it made me uncomfortable that Valerie was even asking. The last thing I needed was Oscar Knight getting too curious about my skills. It could prevent me from using them when they were really needed.

I walked to the door and beckoned Valerie, softening the eviction with a smile. "I wish I'd been able to give you some advice, but we'll be sure to stop in soon."

Her posture drooped as she accepted the tub of bran muffins from Ren. "Please do. Free coffee for the first week." Remembering how Mitzy died, she added, "Just regular brewed coffee. Nothing fancy."

"Sounds great," I said. "We'll be there with bells on."

The little doorbell overhead made a strange noise as I pulled on the doorknob. Valerie looked up, startled, and stumbled as she left, sending a few bran muffins rolling onto the sidewalk.

"Was that a cackle?" she asked.

I pointed to the birds swooping down from the roof to feast on the muffins. "Just pigeons. You've made their day."

Bixby struggled to get down and then chased the birds away. "We've got enough pests, living or dead," he said, coming back satisfied. "Gotta draw the line somewhere."

CHAPTER THREE

"It's probably nothing, right?" Ren said, as we all walked the few blocks to the Beanstalk Café after Whimsy closed at five.

"Probably," I said. "What are the chances of Mitzy Lennox hanging around?"

"Maybe Mitzy had nowhere else to go," Mr. Bixby said. "Or else limbo was better than the alternative."

He was moving under his own steam for a change. While the dog claimed to prefer walking to being carried, I noticed he was more likely to insist when Bijou was with us. The two had a mostly friendly competition. Aside from slinging snarky remarks at each other, they pretty much pulled together, and literally, when they were both on lead. Neither was large but they had hauling power.

"Mitzy wasn't *that* bad," I said. "I mean, she was a bully but we've met worse. Far worse."

Bixby stopped pulling to stare at me. "She accepted a commission to put you out of commission. Permanently. How much worse does it need to be?"

"Point taken. But she didn't actually follow through, which means she may have had redeeming qualities."

Ren's eyes had a glazed look. "Do I want to know how all this ghost stuff works?"

"Probably not, and luckily I can't even tell you. I can count the ghosts I've met on one hand and all of them are quality folk, whether human or canine."

Sinda turned to me. "I've often wondered why Sir Nigel stuck around when he should have a free pass to wherever good people go."

"Me too," I said. "His sense of duty seems to bind him here, even though every Brighton, including Mom, has encouraged him to... well, enjoy a well-earned retirement. He gets quite offended, actually."

"As would I," Mr. Bixby said. "We're all entitled to our choices, whether or not others understand them."

"I'm grateful for yours, Bixby. Even though you're about to break my fingers."

We were moving at quite a clip, but it didn't stop me from enjoying the sights as dusk fell over Main Street. Many preferred spring or summer in Wyldwood but I'd always loved the fall colors. The vines that climbed walls or spilled over balconies had turned scarlet, and planters fairly exploded with chrysanthemums in gold, orange and maroon.

"Do you really think Mitzy might be haunting the Beanstalk?" Ren asked, slowing despite Bijou's momentum. "I'd rather not see her again. She bullied me in life and I hate to think about how she might build on that now."

"I bet it's nothing at all," I said. "Valerie understandably has a bad case of nerves."

"Why on earth would she take over a store so recently vacated in such a way?" Sinda said.

I tried to slow down, but after a short stint of raiding Mom's wardrobe, I was back to wearing my own stilettos and they didn't really come with brakes. That was probably half the battle in staying ahead of trouble all those years I rolled from resort to resort working in hospitality. At the first hint of magical trouble, I shifted those heels into overdrive.

"I can see why she would," Ren said. "I dreamed of opening a bakery here for years but it wasn't in the realm of possibility until Janelle came home."

Bending, I scooped up my dashing doxy while his paws were still pumping. "And it was only possible for me because of some fancy footwork with Oscar Knight." Bijou had helped me figure out that Oscar's son, Jared, had framed me for a murder he committed. "Plus the generosity of Sinda, Gran and Mom in making our down payment."

"I invested in all of us," Sinda said. "Couldn't be happier about it."

We slowed as we neared the café. "I empathize with Valerie," I said. "She's where we were until recently. And now that she's caught an unexpected break, there may be strings attached."

"If you do find Mitzy Lennox in there waiting tables, what do you plan to do about it?" Mr. Bixby asked.

I stared into space, pondering. "Ask her politely to leave?"

"Even your family ghost won't move on despite a few nudges in the celestial direction." The dog squirmed under my arm. "Mitzy wasn't open to suggestions in life, unlike your butler."

"How about we play this by ear?" Sinda said, as we lined up outside the café and stared through the window. "It may not be haunted at all."

It was, though.

Just not by Mitzy.

CHAPTER FOUR

The Beanstalk Café had changed very little since I was a child. Until today, I hadn't realized how well the interior design suited autumn, with rust-colored wainscoting, brown hardwood floors and booths with green and gold upholstery. There were round bistro tables with wooden chairs, and several stools lined up in front of the long counter.

What really set the café apart from any other I'd seen—and I'd seen hundreds of them—was the library. The built-in shelves in front of the counter held books instead of coffee beans or other products. They were classics, as I knew well, and that's probably what kept them from being stolen. Some were well-worn but others pristine. Gran used to bring me here after school for a milkshake and we worked our way through at least a dozen of them. It was her way of balancing a treat with something healthy.

I hoped Valerie would keep the little library that had predated Mitzy's ownership but I grew more skeptical as we walked inside. Several books were lying on the floor, and as I watched, a large white dog with gorgeous feathers and a heavy sprinkling of black freckles added another hardcover to the pile.

"Oh, for pity's sake, it's another ghost," Mr. Bixby said. "What is it this time? A Dalmatian with pretensions?"

"I think it's an English setter." I could have used our inside communication channel but Ren and Sinda were staring at the dog, too. At one time I was the only one who could see these canine specters, but as our powers grew, that was something we shared. "The breed isn't common anymore. At least not around these parts."

"So pretty," Ren murmured. "I've never seen one before."

Valerie Fairchild's eyes lit up and she came around the counter to escort us to a table as if we were royalty. There wasn't much competition for seating, unfortunately. Only one other table was taken. An old man in a trench coat and fedora was hunched over a newspaper near the wall.

"I've barely had a customer all day," she whispered, as we got settled. "I suppose I can't blame anyone after what happened. I don't even know why I said yes when Mr. Knight called." She glanced around and sighed. "My lips tried to say no but yes came out."

"Oscar has that effect on people," I said. "He's a hard man to turn down."

She took our order and then forced a smile. "Guess he'll be the one saying no soon enough. At the rate I'm going, I won't be able to cover the rent."

"Give it a fair chance," Ren said. "We'll spread the word, I promise."

Valerie thanked her and headed back to the counter. She stopped to put the fallen books on the shelf. I knew they were out of order. There was a mental image in my mind of exactly how those books should be filed.

"Your backing would probably hurt Valerie more than help," Mr. Bixby said, from my lap. "Like it or not, you're associated in people's minds with Mitzy's death. Promoting her successor would be the height of—"

"Kindness, short stuff," Bijou said, popping up from Ren's lap. "If you don't have anything nice to say—"

"Then I would always be silent," he replied. "And not doing my job as Janelle's companion."

To Valerie's credit, she hadn't complained when we brought the dogs in, or even asked us about therapy designation. That said a lot about her, and possibly explained why the ghost dog had taken up residence. The new owner must have a kind heart.

"Maybe that feathery beast was always here and just didn't come out till now," Bixby said.

The English setter caught my eye and then pawed another book off the shelf. It seemed like a defiant move. Attention seeking.

"Look at the cheek on her," Bixby added.

"Him," I said. "Atticus, I believe. No wonder he has a literary bent. *To Kill a Mockingbird* was one of my all-time favorite books. Gran and I read it together here, sometimes at this very table."

"That's a beautiful memory," Sinda said, getting up to replace the book before Valerie saw it. "With Mitzy gone, maybe you can reclaim the place."

When she sat down again, I asked her to check her records to see if there was an English setter among the ghost dog jewelry collection. Seeing the photo on her phone was more of a formality by this point. The dog was letting me know he was available for business. Unfortunately, bringing a ghost back wasn't as easy as flipping a switch. A whole bunch of elements needed to line up before I could arrange for his transport into this plane of existence. In my experience, I had control over very few of them, or at least not until the last moment.

"I am not on board for this," Mr. Bixby said. "Nor is Bijou."

I thought the poodle might disagree but she stared at the bigger dog and then disappeared under the table again. Perhaps the two small dogs feared getting lost in the shuffle as our pack grew. That would never happen, but Atticus would probably make some dog lover very happy. Hopefully not any time soon, as every similar rescue had cost a lot in terms of time and stress. In fact, every similar rescue had involved a murder.

The white freckled dog kept his eyes on mine as he pulled out yet another book. He didn't even care which one he was clawing.

"Stop that," I said, shaking my finger. "Those books are treasures, not toys."

I was still wagging my finger when the door opened and Maisie Gledhill walked into the café. Ren and I had landed on her bad side during my first days back in town, and Mom had gotten the ball rolling even sooner. Maisie was probably around 80 and had hair so closely cropped I suspected she used a razor. Her plaid shirt, jeans and dirty boots confirmed vanity wasn't among her failings.

Nor was courtesy among her virtues, as attested by her scowl when she saw us. "A Brighton," she said. "I thought I smelled trouble."

Mr. Bixby sat up and yapped insults in regular dog language. I shushed him with a silent reminder that Maisie had good reason to detest us. She'd caught us trespassing in her greenhouse, just as she had Mom. The horrible things she said about my family that night still rankled.

"Hi, Maisie," Ren said. "I don't think you'll find your favorite strawberry mousse cake here. At least, not yet."

"You can try Ren's bakery when it opens next week," I said. "Flour Girl."

Maisie snorted. "Neither of you could pay me to darken your doors after stealing valuable plants from me."

"Do you have proof of that, Mrs. Gledhill?" I asked. "I've heard your claims but they were never proven."

Maisie tapped her shaved scalp. "I have all the proof I need that you girls are a big problem in Wyldwood. Everyone knows it."

Valerie stood on the other side of the counter wringing her hands. "What can I get you, madam?"

"If I had a choice, I'd walk out empty-handed because of your clientele," Maisie said. "But I'm hosting my granddaughter's bridal shower. Give me a dozen cupcakes. Stat."

"I heard Brianna is getting married," Ren said. "I've always liked her. And she liked my rocky road brownies."

"Just stop, Renata. I see right through you. You and your friends have tainted the place, so this will be my last visit." Maisie stared around. "I really just came by to see it one last time before the ship sinks."

Valerie looked as if she'd taken a hard kick from Maisie's muddy work boot. "I'm sorry to hear that," she said, putting cupcakes into a box.

I shook my head. "Mrs. Gledhill, would it kill you to be nice? Valerie deserves a fighting chance to make her business a success."

"That'll be up to Oscar Knight, I assume," Maisie said. "She's just one of many puppets in his Wyldwood show, isn't she?"

The English setter pulled out another book, which fell on the floor with a thud that startled Maisie.

"You scared the books right off the shelf, Mrs. Gledhill," I said, trying to catch Mr. Bixby as he slid off my lap like a sleek otter. He had become invisible and eluded my fingers.

I could tell he was trotting directly at Maisie, however, simply by tracking the tall white dog's muzzle. He could apparently see Mr. Bixby when the rest of us could not.

"Ow!" Maisie jumped and turned quickly. "Something just bit me."

"Bit you?" Valerie said, eyes widening.

"In the back of the calf." Maisie craned to see her leg. "Through my jeans. Do you have an infestation here?"

"Of course not," Valerie said.

Maisie jumped again. "Oh yes, you do. Is it any wonder after someone died here? I think Mitzy Lennox passed away right where you're standing."

"You're wrong, Maisie." I got up and walked over. "Ren and I were here when the police arrived."

The old woman spun as she tried to evade invisible teeth. "Not something to boast about, either of you. You're bad luck, Janelle Brighton, and I'm going to leave while I still can."

She had help from behind and was soon on her way, carrying a box of cupcakes that probably wouldn't arrive in great shape.

It might have been funny, if not for the look of utter despair on Valerie Fairchild's face. "This whole thing is turning into a cosmic joke," she said.

I snapped my fingers to get my invisible dog to heel, which was a joke in and of itself. Bixby rarely followed commands, and certainly not a finger snap.

"Insulting," he said, in my head. "I used my judgement in banning Maisie from the place. Use *yours* in dealing with Mr. Tall, White and Feathery."

"Valerie, don't worry," I said. "We're going to help."

"With the ghost?" she asked, brightening. "What are you going to do?"

"There are worse problems than a ghost," I said. "Luckily, we like a challenge."

"Glad there's free coffee for a week," Mr. Bixby said. He materialized at my feet, out of Valerie's range of vision, and then sauntered back to the table. "You're going to need it."

CHAPTER FIVE

I sent my friends home to the manor so that I could spend some time alone studying the new ghost dog. It was only seven, but the flickering traffic lights outside made it seem later. Soon, the town would truly light up for Christmas. Since I was on the planning committee with Oscar Knight and Mayor Ruthann Longmuir, I knew that would happen two days after Thanksgiving.

I wasn't actually alone. Mr. Bixby sat on the upholstered bench beside me, grumbling pretty much nonstop at Atticus, the ghostly English setter. I had been in the Beanstalk Café many times since coming home and there was no doubt in my mind I'd have noticed this dog. He was utterly stunning and his mischievous streak told me he very much wanted to be noticed. The fact that he kept knocking books off the shelf—books I loved—told me he wanted to be noticed by me, in particular.

Atticus was a new arrival and his presence meant something.

"You can't go chasing after meaning in every ghost dog in this town," Mr. Bixby said. "There must be hundreds of them."

"Possibly, but I keep my eyes open and this is only the third ghost dog I've met in Wyldwood. I assume they want to be seen."

More specifically, I assumed they wanted to come back, either to finish some business, like Harold, or start something new, like Bixby and Bijou. At this point, it didn't feel right to question their motives. All of the ghost dogs I'd met had noble callings.

"So far," Bixby said. "I don't imagine it'll stay that way when word gets out. Which it clearly is. We barely had two weeks clear before the next one showed its ugly face."

I laughed, earning a curious look from Valerie, who was brewing a fresh pot of coffee for me. A latte would have been nice but I didn't blame her for not replacing the old espresso machine after what happened with Mitzy Lennox. Most people in town thought the former owner had died of electrocution by way of a faulty appliance. It was more a case of execution by way of a corrupt warlock.

"I thought we didn't use the 'w' words," Mr. Bixby said. "Specifically, witch, warlock and wiener dog. Are we casting the lexicon of forbidden words aside just because Liberty mocked it?"

I shook my head as I stroked his sleek flanks. "Liberty's managed to mock nearly everything we hold dear in her short time here. We can't let her opinions hold us back."

"Yet here you sit in your own sharp dress and heels, after she dismissed your mother's borrowed finery."

I had indeed worn Mom's unfashionable clothes for a time after coming home. It had felt like a disguise and even offered a measure of comfort. "Okay, fine. If Liberty happens to state what I already know, I take it under advisement. But she hasn't presented convincing evidence I'm a you-know-what."

"If not that, then what?" he asked, chuckling.

"Just another young person finding herself." My laugh was rueful. "I hoped that search would end before I turned thirty."

"Still young by my estimation," he said.

Valerie came over with a steaming mug of coffee and thanked me again for staying. I figured we'd get into a longer conversation but someone else came through the door and she had to go back to the counter. At least the café was getting customers.

Mr. Bixby poked his head up to stare at Atticus. "Can you make your point so we can get on with our live? I forfeited my evening walk because of you."

"He's forfeited a lot more than that, I'm sure," I said, using our inside channel. "You would know that better than I do."

Mr. Bixby subsided into huffy silence. He didn't really like talking about his time as a ghost dog or how he ended up in that situation. I assumed he'd made a choice along the way. Perhaps turned back at the pearly gates or the rainbow bridge, or whatever route dogs took after they passed. Maybe he'd taken a vow of silence, because little else could shut this dog up.

"Just focus on the problem at hand," he said. "In case you hadn't noticed, there's one of the human variety coming in for a landing."

I barely had time to find a bland smile before a woman pulled out the chair opposite mine and sat down with her back to the door. Like the old man reading the paper, she was wearing a trench coat. Her hair was covered with a bright silk scarf, and despite the late hour, she was wearing oversized sunglasses.

There was something familiar about her but the disguise threw me off.

"Think snakes," Bixby said. "His better half."

It wouldn't be hard to be better than Oscar Knight, but his wife, Octavia, had struck me as very congenial when she visited Whimsy on opening day. Cousin Liberty had accosted her about Oscar's misdeeds and Octavia had responded by buying nearly all my stock.

And now she was sitting across from me when there were a dozen other tables entirely free.

"Good evening, Mrs. Knight," I said. "Are you undercover? Checking the place out for Oscar?"

She lifted her glasses to expose clear blue eyes and then dropped them again, frowning. "Am I that obvious?"

I smiled and gestured to Bixby. "A little dog told me."

"Not that little," he said, jerking his head toward the ghost dog, who was back at his post near the bookshelf. "Not that big, either."

"Your dachshund is adorable," Mrs. Knight said. "It almost sounds like he's talking, with those grumble-mumbles."

"I know, right? Believe it or not, I can practically understand him."

The glasses came up again. Her eyes looked slightly puffy, perhaps from crying. "I heard you were a genius with dogs."

My laughter was drowned out by Mr. Bixby's, but she could only hear mine. "Not really. Not even a genius with *this* dog, come to think of it. But I couldn't ask for a better companion. I'm sure you feel the same about your Rhodesian ridgeback."

"My Philomena." The glasses fell like shutters. "Very much so, yes. That's actually why I'm here."

I stared at her opaque lenses. "You're at the Beanstalk to talk to me about your dog?"

"Well, I couldn't take the chance of Oscar or his men seeing me at Whimsy. He was so upset about what happened."

"About the charge you racked up on opening day? Because you can absolutely return your purchases, Mrs. Knight."

Reaching out, she squeezed my wrist. Since I was holding the full mug, I couldn't move my hand quickly enough. Drive-by grabs were something I normally avoided because I didn't welcome unsolicited psychic input from relative strangers. However, Mrs. Knight's touch wasn't nearly as alarming as her husband's. She was certainly agitated—even scared—but there was nothing menacing, at least in what I called "the foyer" of her mind. My skills were still rudimentary enough that I needed far more time and just the right circumstances to dive much deeper.

"You'd have moved beyond rudimentary by now if you hadn't decided to specialize in ghost dogs," Mr. Bixby said. "It's rather limiting, don't you think? Unless you're looking to replace me."

"Never." I sent the single word of reassurance before easing my wrist out of Mrs. Knight's grasp. It took some doing, given the steaming liquid threatening to spill over the mug's brim.

"It's not about what I bought at the store," she said. "It's about what Liberty said. Oscar is livid. He's worried she's splashing rumors around."

"Cousin Liberty is down south with my gran and Mom, and she didn't have time to reconnect with old friends before going. As far as I can tell, she's not particularly interested in gossip, Mrs. Knight. I hear Liberty's always marched to her own drummer."

She tried to grab my wrist again, so I released the mug and dropped my hands into my lap. For all I knew she might infect me with a spell from Oscar. I had discovered on my own that they could be passed along like viruses.

"Janelle, please. I need your help."

Taking the glasses right off, she set them on the table. Then she grabbed my mug and chugged the entire contents. The brew must have burned her lips and tongue but she seemed oblivious.

"What's the problem, Octavia?"

She glanced around quickly, eyes lighting briefly on the old man. "Call me Tavi. Everyone does."

"Well, Tavi then. How can I help?"

"Don't be too hasty," Bixby said. "It's probably a trap."

It may well have been, but she was putting on a good act.

She leaned in very close. "I've left Oscar. Or rather, I've asked him to leave. For the moment he's living in the pool house. It'll get mighty cold out there soon, though."

Her face was close enough I could smell her breath. Despite the coffee she drank, minty freshness enveloped me.

"That's what toothpaste is for," Bixby said. "Temporary masking. Oscar doesn't bother because he likes people to feel faint in his presence."

Ignoring him, I met the woman's eyes. "You threw Oscar out because of his spell on Cousin Liberty?"

"No! Well, I mean, yes, that too. But there will always be feuds in this town and Liberty could be a bit grating. No offense to your family."

"I haven't known her long, but I doubt anything she did or said was worth cursing her and leaving her to die a slow death in her own home. And worse, about Harold—"

She held up a manicured hand. "Don't. I can't bear hearing it again. What he did to that dog was unconscionable."

"That's why he's in the pool house?"

"Exactly. If he did that to Harold, he has put my precious Philomena at risk. Liberty will want revenge. That's the Wyldwood way."

I leaned back in my chair. The minty freshness made me a little lightheaded. "I'm new to Wyldwood ways, Mrs. Knight, and even new to my cousin Liberty. But I know without a shadow of a doubt that she would never harm your dog. One of the first things she said after recovering was that we have a love of dogs in common."

She leaned back, too, and I felt the waves of anxiety ebbing. "Still, I'd feel better if there was a protective spell around Philomena."

"That makes sense." In fact, I should have thought of it before. Why didn't I have a shield around Bixby and Bijou?

"Because we're exceptional?" he said. "Especially me. Oscar might try his funny business but he'd fail."

An uneasy feeling churned in my stomach along with the single mouthful of coffee I'd downed before Tavi drank the rest. What if Oscar did try? Mr. Bixby was alive now. Alive with something extra, yes, but did that make him impervious to all bad magic? And now that Oscar knew Liberty's weakness for dogs, which I just happened to share, wouldn't that be exactly how he sought revenge on me for past grudges? Maybe his wife already knew his plan.

"I need your help to do this, Janelle," she said.

"To do what?" Bixby said, before I could. "Tuck Philomena into magical bubble wrap?"

"Mrs. Knight," I said. "Tavi. You must know I'm already a frequent target of your husband's ire. Just for being a Brighton, for starters."

Her fine eyebrows rose. "Plus tricking him into selling you the stores."

"That too, I suppose." I wasn't sure how much he'd told her. Surely she knew about her son Jared's involvement in the high school crime that still tarnished my name—the one he committed and Oscar covered up.

"My husband feels strongly about real estate," she said. "And even I can admit he's ruthless in business."

"Exactly, and he still wants to put *me* out of business, so I can't risk annoying him even more."

"I'll pay you well, Janelle. Very well. At the moment, Oscar hasn't locked me out of the accounts, so we should move fast."

"Pay me? To do what?"

"To cast the spell, of course." Splaying her hands on the table, she added, "And to get the rangleroot."

"I don't understand. Why would you need me to do that for you?"

Her long lashes batted a few times and then tears splashed over. "Because I'm magically challenged. You must have heard that. Everyone talks about how Oscar married beneath him."

I knew Jared had no magical abilities but it hadn't occurred to me that he'd inherited that from his mother. In fact, I didn't believe it now. When I was in her mental "foyer," I sensed something. It wasn't the roiling magical snakes her husband embodied, but she was not without a spark of power.

"Tavi, I think you underestimate yourself. Perhaps you're just a late bloomer."

"Very late," she said, finding a small smile. "I'm nearly sixty, Janelle."

"It happens. I know from personal experience."

She shook her head hard. "It won't happen to me. I'm a... Well, a dud is the term most commonly used."

I flinched, having heard it too often myself. "They called me that, too. Magic isn't always obvious, and if we're invested in keeping it under wraps, well... people get the wrong impression."

"It's worse to have a little than none at all," she said. "Except in a case like this. If I could protect Philomena myself, I would. But I know you'll help." Pointing at Bixby, she added, "You can cover your wonderful dachshund at the same time. And your friend's poodle, too. I'm sure Liberty's already secured Harold."

A thudding sound made us both turn. Two books lay on the floor under the shelf. Atticus tipped his head and repeatedly offered me a paw. His feathery tail thumped briskly on the floor.

All signs indicated that the ghost dog endorsed Tavi's idea.

"Your living dog disagrees, however," Mr. Bixby said. "Janelle, you're not a witch for hire, and yes, in this one instance, I'll use that word. Oscar warned you it was dangerous to get between a man and his wife and in general, I'd have to agree. There's more going on here than meets the eye."

"I know. You're right."

I said the words out loud and Octavia thought I was talking to her. "I knew you'd see it my way. Rangleroot is very hard to find. You'll need to buy it from Maisie Gledhill."

"Maisie! She won't sell it to me. In fact, sending me there is the surest way *not* to get it. You must know others who are better connected."

"Better connected to my husband, you mean. Oscar has always kept me very sheltered."

"For your own safety, I presume. If you want to protect Philomena, imagine how he feels about you. That's probably why he's still staying in the pool house in cold weather. He could afford a hotel."

Pressing her lips together, she sat in silence for a few moments. "I'm like a bird in a cage," she said, at last. "The only thing that keeps me sane is Philomena. So, please help me protect her by getting hold of that rangleroot by whatever means possible. I'll make it worth your while."

"I don't want your money, Mrs. Knight."

"Tavi," she repeated. "I didn't figure you would, but at least I have the spell you need to protect Mr. Bixby. Isn't that worth something?"

"A spell from Oscar's book? He'll know how to break it."

She got to her feet and adjusted her scarf. "From my mother's book. She used it to keep my brother and me safe when we were kids. Rangleroot was even harder to find back then, before Maisie got her business going. An obnoxious woman, but there's no denying her green thumb. She's made a killing from it." Dropping the shades onto the bridge of her nose once more, she added, "Poor choice of words."

My head was shaking but before I could say the word no, Tavi was on the move. I don't know if she thanked me out loud but I heard it anyway.

Atticus raised his paw in a sedate point, which made me look down at the table. Oscar's wife had left something behind.

Three things, actually.

A folded piece of paper, and her engagement and wedding rings.

CHAPTER SIX

Renata's skills with a machete had improved markedly since the first time we hacked through the bush to Maisie Gledhill's greenhouse in the dark. Something else had changed, too. Bijou had been a ghost bound to the store, then. Now, she was ahead of Ren every step of the way, sniffing for trouble. The poodle's protests formed a stream of consciousness tirade that was harder to penetrate than the bush, although Mr. Bixby kept trying to get a word in edgewise.

Finally, in a particularly knotty section, he said, "I want to state my objections for the record. In case you ladies failed to notice the first few times."

"I didn't," I said, stumbling along in Ren's wake. Despite how busy we were, she had found time to do some wilderness training with Edna Evans, an aging prepper who'd become close to my cousin, Jilly Blackwood, and her best friend Ivy Galloway. Ren and Sinda had been up to visit them at Runaway Farm twice for private tutoring. Nonetheless, Sinda had elected to stay back and guard our stores tonight. We didn't know if we were hacking into a trap.

"Oh, you are," Mr. Bixby said. "I have no doubt about that.

Agreeing to help Oscar Knight's wife is a suicide mission. Only you're taking the rest of us down with you."

He made his argument aloud in hopes that Ren and Bijou would take his side. I figured they should hear it, too. "I'm not helping his wife, per se, but her dog. Plus my own dog, and Ren's."

He struggled in my arms but he didn't really want to get down and fight through the bush. "You can't trust someone who's been married to that snake for over thirty years. Whether she knows it or not, she's been weaponized. He probably planted a spell bomb in her."

"Maybe, but I don't think so," I said. "I've got her rings, and stones don't lie. Especially sapphire. For me, that's a truth stone. At the very least, Octavia believes what she's saying."

"Which means little as far as Oscar is concerned. Do you really think he'd stop at tampering with his wife's brain?"

"Hard to say, but I believe he adores and wants to protect Tavi. Those stones were packed with images of him doting on her."

So much so, that holding them left me feeling like a shameless voyeur. The impressions made me question what I knew about Oscar. However, Tavi herself had acknowledged her husband could be ruthless in business.

"I still don't get it," Mr. Bixby said. "Why you? She can afford to get anyone to do this for her. Plenty of people would be happy to take her money."

I pushed a heavy branch out of the way before answering. "I wish she had, Bixby, really I do. I can only assume it's because Ren and I managed to break into Maisie's greenhouse before. She knows that through Oscar. Plus we've outwitted his schemes. Few can say that."

"Maisie will have increased security since then," he said. "Octavia is willingly letting you risk your life for the sake of her dog."

"She cares that much about Philomena. The rings confirmed it."

"There has to be another way. Did you ask your mom? Liberty?" He grunted in frustration. "Oh wait, no, you just charged out into the night without a second thought."

"Not true. I changed my clothes and gave Ren time to collect the tools she needed."

Finally Ren stopped hacking to join the discussion. "Mr. Bixby, we're doing it. The more you distract us, the more likely we are to be caught."

"Renata, you disappoint me. Normally you're the voice of reason."

She smiled, her white teeth gleaming in the faint light from the phone in my pocket. "Not where Bijou is concerned, Bixby. I want to make sure she's protected, just like Janelle does you."

"The spell Octavia shared is probably rigged," he said. "It could turn us into turnips. Or worse."

"Atticus didn't think so," I said. "He wanted us to do it."

The dachshund let his head flop dramatically over my arm. "Another ghost dog with big opinions. You only met him today, and you trust him?"

"Like I trusted you within seconds of meeting you. Dogs come to me for a reason."

"All Atticus did was toss old books around. And you read all that into it?" His head lifted as he appreciated his unintended joke. "Surely the message is open to interpretation, just like every work of literature."

I remembered how I hated English classes, where we were supposed to find great truths in books. The notion of "theme" always evaded me and I wondered if authors had any idea about what teachers would see in their published works. There was a good reason I dropped out of college, other than being framed for arson. I was never meant to be a scholar.

"You're smart enough," Bixby said. "Except for the extreme stupidity of this particular moment."

"Let's just get it done," I said. "Maisie will be busy with the bridal shower and it's the perfect time."

The dog snorted. "Really? There's no such thing as a perfect time to get caught in one of Maisie Gledhill's snares. Furthermore, I won't stand around waiting for you to fire a spell at me that isn't at the very least covered in *Everyday Spells for Everyday Magic*. That's setting the bar quite low, in my opinion."

"My spell book once belonged to Cousin Liberty," I reminded him, forging ahead. "It can't be that bad."

He continued to grumble. "It can't be that good, or she wouldn't have been felled by Oscar Knight."

"And his cronies, don't forget. Besides, it was magic from that book—Liberty's beginner's manual—that broke his spell."

"Thanks to me."

I laughed. "Thanks to you, yes. Which is why I need to do my very best to protect you, Mr. Bixby, so that you can continue to protect me. Not only from Oscar and his crew, but my own misguided family."

He sniffed huffily again but the outrage notched down from a 10 to an eight. "I still refuse to be subjected to Octavia Knight's mystery spell. She said she wants you to cast it on Philomena, so I suppose we'll see what happens."

"How about we cross that bridge when we come to it? There won't be any spelling if we can't get the rangleroot."

I hoped he'd settle for that but his brain was overflowing. "What we need is a magical committee to review all spells under consideration."

Ren glanced back. "There's an idea. Who'd lead it? Shelley or Liberty?"

"Liberty, I suppose," Bixby said. "She's the senior witch, although they're equally unpredictable."

"I like your idea," I said. "How about we run this spell by both

Mom and Liberty? If they approve, we go for it. If not, we just hand the rangleroot over to Tavi Knight."

That finally turned off his chat switch and he was quiet until the trees started to thin out. Then he started up again with requests to be set down, and I was glad to release him.

"Bicker, bicker, bicker," Bijou said. "All work for us, all play for you."

He flounced past her. "I wasn't built for work, poodle. Unless you call hunting vermin work, which I do not."

"Pretty much all you work is your mouth, wiener boy," she said, getting ahead of him again.

Technically, their mouths didn't actually work, although there was plenty of vocalization others could hear. Those with an ear for "dog" could always pick up their general tone, but only Ren, Sinda, Mom and Liberty could follow the conversation.

It wasn't long before Mr. Bixby raised more objections. "So, you're going to cast a non-sanctioned spell on Tavi's non-magical dog? Isn't that irresponsible?"

I scooped him up again as we approached the fence bordering Maisie's property. "We don't know anything about Philomena but she seemed nice enough the day we met Oscar in the park. I feel like I have a duty to protect regular dogs just as much as magical ones."

He flopped dramatically yet again, suddenly seeming several pounds heavier than a dachshund could possibly be. "Where will this end?"

"For now, it ends here," Ren said. "I hadn't expected to see the place again so soon, but I must say I feel better than last time around."

She looked better, too, as I pulled out my phone light. We'd been in crazy disguises on our first visit to Maisie's greenhouse, whereas this time we'd gone with basic black and balaclavas. There was also more pep in our step because we were no longer being poisoned. Just the thought of how miserable we'd felt made me throw back my shoulders and pull in a big breath of frosty air. The stars overhead were pale pinpricks in a black drop cloth. I had thought they'd be brighter here in Wyldwood, but the opposite seemed to be true. Maybe all the magic created a haze, like pollution.

"You have time to contemplate the big dipper?" Mr. Bixby asked, as Ren scaled the fence.

Once her boots were safely on the ground, I passed over Bijou and then Bixby. He objected to the order of priority but I tuned him out.

"Do you think the greenhouse is rigged?" Ren asked, as Bixby took the lead and trotted toward it. "I mean, *more* rigged?"

The last time we got in without mishap but tripped alarms and got trapped inside. We'd escaped with a little magic and a lot of luck. Maisie suspected it was us but she had no proof. Still, I'd expected her to take action against us. Maybe she didn't want the police to know exactly what she was growing on the premises. There was a reason Mom had broken in, and a reason Octavia sent us here. Maisie clearly had the best flora in town.

"I would think so," I said. "We'll need to be on the lookout."

"For what, exactly?" Ren scratched her head through the balaclava. "Are there magical clues I don't know about?"

I shrugged. "Something else to ask Liberty when she takes over our new committee. For the moment, all we can do is study what's changed."

Something very obvious had changed, as it turned out. The glass door to the greenhouse had been locked the last time. Now it was not only unlocked but wide open. On closer inspection, I saw it was crooked and the upper hinge was broken.

Shattered, actually. There were bits of metal scattered on the earth that mirrored the stars in the sky, only brighter.

"Well, that's odd," Ren whispered, stopping a few feet away.

"It's gotta be a trick. We walk through the open door and a net comes down, right?"

"Or a web of dark magic," I said. "Next thing you know Maisie's feeding us to the Venus flytraps, bit by bit."

"Maybe she's genetically modified one of those to handle bigger prey," Ren said. "They're always looking for places to stow the bodies in this town."

It was tempting to stand around cracking jokes, but we couldn't afford to linger. "I guess we should do something. But we can't just walk in there like it's a public garden."

Bixby put a paw on my foot to get my attention. "I'll do it. You're a couple of shrinking violets."

Before I could argue, he became invisible.

Ren moved closer to me. "Can magic harm him when he's like that?"

"No," Bixby said, prancing through the door. I couldn't actually *see* him prancing, of course, but I could tell from his tone. "And for your information, Janelle... dachshunds don't prance."

His voice transitioned to my head, and then faded as he got distracted.

"I don't know much about invisibility in general, or Bixby's ability in particular," I told Ren. "Something else to ask Liberty."

"She doesn't seem like the type to sit down with beginners," Ren said. "In fact, the only time she took notice of me was when she wanted a coffee or snack. Modern appliances might be the only things that intimidate her."

Bijou urged us to be quiet and we obeyed. This way, I could hear Bixby's commentary in my head as he surveilled the greenhouse. He already knew his way around.

"Everything is as it was, so far," he said. "I can smell the rangleroot, although I object on principle to using it for the spell you have in mind."

"We'll run it by Liberty, I promise," I told him, still silently.

"Janelle..." He started to speak and then stopped.

"I mean it, Bixby. From now on, we run all magical decisions past Liberty."

There was a strategic pause, at which point he continued. "I've changed my mind about getting her input."

"Why? Cousin Liberty's the best woman for the job."

"Let's see if you still think so in five minutes," he said.

There was mumbling at his end.

"Mr. Bixby? Who are you talking to?"

"Liberty," he said. "She's right here."

"In the greenhouse? Why?"

"Ask her. All I can say is she's not my first choice to lead the committee anymore. Or anything else."

CHAPTER SEVEN

Renata, Bijou and I rushed into the greenhouse without waiting for Bixby's signal to advance. If Liberty was inside, it must be safe.

"Not exactly," the dog said, still out of earshot. "Do be careful."

I explained the situation to Ren as best I could. "Bixby says it's not safe."

"Well," he continued in my head, "it might be safe for you. It wasn't safe for everyone."

We ran from row to row, looking for Liberty, since we couldn't see the dog. "What do you mean?" I asked him.

"Slow down," he said, out loud now. "Use your phone light."

"No lights," someone else said. It sounded like Cousin Liberty... at least, sort of. Since she'd recovered, her voice had been robust and confident, whereas tonight, it was wispy. Uncertain.

"Cousin Liberty," I said, starting up a row. "What's going on?"

I could see her standing at the midway point. There was enough light from a bank of fluorescents over a table of plants at the back of the greenhouse. Her hair was in her usual elegant braided coronet and she was most certainly in heels, judging by her height. Unlike us, she hadn't come for a raid. Or at least, hadn't dressed for a raid.

"There's a bit of a problem," she said. "I was just deciding what to do about it."

"More than a bit," Mr. Bixby said. "And I suggest you think fast, madam."

I stared around for telltale signs of wind. "Where's Harold?"

The only wind came from her rather gusty sigh. "I sent him to secure the perimeter."

"From Maisie? Does she know you're here?"

The faint light glinted off her hair as she shook her head. "She didn't, actually."

"Didn't? Past tense?" A little chill ran down my spine. But it wasn't like the past tense was always permanent. There was no reason to think so now.

"Except there is," Mr. Bixby said. "I'm the one on eye level with Maisie."

I had reached them and my dachshund, now visible, was standing beside Maisie Gledhill's prostrate form. "Did she pass out?" I asked. My voice was hopeful but my mind was registering an absence where Maisie's energy should be. There was a void, where only hours ago, she'd crackled with life. It was the first time I realized I could sense such things without actually touching someone. What an unfortunate way to discover growing abilities.

"She passed right out of existence," Mr. Bixby said. "And there's no time for self-reflection, Janelle. Maisie may have tripped an alarm before Liberty tripped her. This place was as secure as the state penitentiary when we visited last time." He crept a little closer to the dead woman. "For what it's worth, Maisie did shave her head."

"A woman's hair is her crowning glory." Liberty's voice was still muted but getting stronger. "Even Maisie's, once upon a time. She was making a statement with that buzzcut, I suppose. Perhaps it made her feel tougher."

"Cousin Liberty," I said, "maybe we could discuss that later. You're standing over Maisie's body."

"Aunt," she said, patting her own hair with fidgety movements.

Edging around the body, I touched Liberty's arm. "Pardon me?"

"*Aunt* Liberty. I don't like 'cousin.' It's too familiar. And great-aunt suggests I'm—"

"Too old to be worrying about labels?" Mr. Bixby suggested.

She glared at him. Well, I read a glare into her posture. I couldn't see her expression. "Old enough to know that familiars should show some respect," she said. "Harold would never speak to me that way."

Mr. Bixby snorted. "Hairball is a dog of few words, but something tells me he warned you against coming tonight."

The step backward confirmed it. "He may have suggested it was a bad idea, yes. But I thought I might surprise Maisie when everyone assumed I was still out of town."

"Looks like you did just that," Mr. Bixby said. "More like *overdid* it."

If he was trying to bring back Liberty's feisty side, the impatient twitch of her hand suggested it was working. "Whatever happened to Maisie tonight, I had no part of it. This is how I found her."

"First you tried the house?" the dog prompted.

Another dismissive flick. "Who are you? Detective Dachshund? I will save my story for Chief Andrew Gillock. You may call him, Janelle. Tell him we're in a spot of trouble over here and would appreciate his discretion."

"Cousin Liberty, I—"

"Aunt Liberty," she corrected. "It sounds so much nicer."

"Liberty," Mr. Bixby interrupted. "You're the one in a spot of trouble. The call would be better coming from you."

"But I'm in shock," she said. "And Janelle has so much more experience with the police."

She was either in shock or denial because both Mom and Gran

told me Liberty had clashes galore with the police before she vanished. At least now she had a fresh set of cops, including the visiting police chief I liked a little too much.

I didn't make the move and finally it was Ren who pulled out her phone. "Someone needs to call and we'll all have some explaining to do."

Liberty's head turned sharply. "That's a very good point, Renata. Why are you girls here?"

"The same reason you are, I presume," I said. "We needed a little something from Maisie's magic garden. Seems like she's the only game in town when it comes to rare flora."

"Not the only one, but the most easily persuaded," Liberty said. "I used to find her amenable, if the price was right."

"Amenable isn't a word I'd use to describe Maisie," I said. "She was—"

"Difficult," Ren interrupted, before stepping away to call the police.

"Obnoxious," Mr. Bixby added.

"Mean, mean, meanie," Bijou concluded.

Liberty tipped her head. "Are you telling me you were just going to help yourselves to something?"

"If you left any," Mr. Bixby said, sniffing around Liberty's heels. "Your purse is stuffed with the rangleroot they want. I know that smell from my days of foraging in the woods. It's so strong I can't smell anything else."

I crossed my arms. "Liberty, did you steal Maisie's rangleroot? All of it? And no, I'm not calling you 'aunt.' I only have one aunt and it's Jilly's mom, Eva."

That earned me a snort. "Eva doesn't even like you. Whereas I am your mentor."

"Well, you did get here ahead of me," I said, as Ren came to stand beside me. "May I ask what you're planning to use the rangleroot for? It's not in the index of your primer, *Everyday Spells for Everyday Magic*."

She rustled around in her purse, perhaps burying the purloined plants under the cosmetics she loved. "It's not easy to come by, obviously, which puts it out of reach for most beginners. Further, it's unpredictable. The concentration of minerals can make or break the spell." Zipping her purse, she stared at me. "Rangleroot is currently beyond your skills, Janelle. How were you planning to use it?"

"A protective spell," I said. "For Bixby and Bijou." I thought about leaving out the rest but if we were to present a united front to the police, full disclosure was better. "And Octavia's Rhodesian ridgeback."

This time the pause felt more shocked than strategic. "Excuse me? Are you saying you have private dealings with Tavi Knight?"

"I guess. She approached me in the Beanstalk Café tonight and asked for my help in protecting her dog. What happened with Harold upset her terribly."

"She's worried her own husband would hurt the dog?"

"And perhaps his many enemies."

Liberty took a step closer. "You had better not be including me on that particular list, Janelle Brighton. I would never harm a hair on any dog's head."

"I told her that but she's been beside herself since you described what happened to Harold. Their marriage is on the rocks and the dog is more important to her than ever."

Liberty started pacing. "I'm not sorry to hear she's getting wise to Oscar. I've known Tavi since she was a child and she deserved better. Oscar took a shine to her early, however, although I don't think their families endorsed the marriage. I've always suspected she wasn't much of a witch, but Oscar is twice the warlock he needs to be."

"To protect her, possibly?" Ren suggested. "It's kind of romantic."

"They've been married thirty years," Liberty said. "Romance never lasts that long."

"Sure it does," Ren said. "My parents are still romantic." She blinked a few times. "I think. I don't see much of them."

"Our kind can't afford romance," Liberty said. "It weakens you. Children weaken you even more."

That was probably true with respect to the Knights' son, Jared, but I couldn't share what I knew with Liberty. She would probably use that knowledge to make things worse. Oscar had threatened Mom's safety if I divulged what I knew, and with Liberty back, it wouldn't stop there.

"That's depressing," Ren said. "But I guess it's nothing in the grand scheme of depressing things this evening."

Liberty had stopped listening to her. "Tavi Knight is a decent sort but you can't trust that you're getting the whole story, Janelle. Why didn't you come to me first?"

"Protect first, ask questions later," Mr. Bixby said. "That's what was driving Janelle. I was pushing for her to run the situation by you, Liberty, but having found you hovering over a body, I must question my own judgement—something I do rarely and with great resentment."

"Spare me, Detective Dachshund," she said, turning at the sound of sirens. "I didn't kill Maisie for a bit of rangleroot I might have found elsewhere with less trouble. But I did take advantage of an open door and no one can blame a witch for that."

"Chiefs Dredger and Gillock probably will," I said.

"That's why you're going to let me do the talking," Liberty said.

With that, she walked over to the greenhouse door and whistled.

CHAPTER EIGHT

Harold, the formerly deceased Australian shepherd I'd brought back for Liberty, created an ear-popping vacuum as he bounded into the greenhouse. He came over to me and wriggled his tailless backside in a greeting before taking his position at Liberty's side. Decades ago, he had died of heartbreak when Oscar committed Liberty to a very slow death via a wasting spell. The dog spent the subsequent years as her ghostly companion, getting around town with the bit of magic she gave him. As a result, when I saved them both, they were so well informed it was as if they had never been gone. The sheepdog's power to move like the wind may have diminished slightly since his return to our plane but he was still far from a typical dog. Only time would tell how the journey back affected all of my ghostly canine rescues.

"Perhaps Janelle should take the lead in the conversation, with my help," Mr. Bixby said. "Chief Gillock wasn't impressed with your style during your last altercation, Liberty."

She pursed her lips. "I'd like to know why the memory spell I cast on him didn't take full effect. Perhaps I wasn't at peak operating capacity after being brought back from the brink. But I sense there's more to it." Raising her eyebrows, she said, "Janelle? Thoughts?"

I shrugged. "All I know is it didn't stick. At least not the way it did with the other officers."

"Were you protecting him?" she asked. "He's a handsome lad and I could understand why. But I need to know."

"I wasn't intentionally doing anything," I said. "But why do you need to know? You can't keep messing with memories. We need to find a better way to handle problems."

"Just let Janelle be," Ren said. "This is all very new to us."

"New gets people killed sooner," Liberty said. "At least Maisie reached eighty. That's old for one of our kind."

Staring in the direction of Maisie's house, her posture shifted. The police must be on the move. "I need to understand your powers so I don't inadvertently affect them with my magic. If I cast a spell on Andrew and you're connected with him in some way, there could be a reverberation."

"So then don't, please. Drew and I haven't even had a date but I like him very much and who knows how that manifests?"

Liberty ran her hands over her hair again and then buttoned her coat. "It's new territory, no question. My psychic powers were rudimentary at best but they've improved considerably since your infusion of power."

"Really?" Mr. Bixby said. "You can thank her for the gift by using the power well."

"It's certainly not a gift to hear what Bridie and Shelley think about me," she said, walking to the doorway. "That's why I had to leave early. I don't know how you stand the constant chatter, Janelle. It's like I can't be alone with my own thoughts." Her fingers reached for Harold. "On the bright side, Harold and I have never been more in sync."

"Interesting," Mr. Bixby said, switching to our inside channel. "If Liberty's absorbed psychic powers from you she never had, what have you picked up from her?"

"I don't even know her special abilities," I said, scooping him up. "Gran and Mom only talked about her eccentricities."

"Obviously she's impulsive and has a temper to get slapped down by Oscar and his cohort," Bixby said. "You were impulsive enough without her contributions."

"Stop talking about me," Liberty said. "Whatever you're saying, it's rude."

I was glad she couldn't read us as easily as Mom, who was a skilled eavesdropper of the psychic kind and pretty shameless about it, too.

Instead of answering, I joined her in the doorway with the dog under my arm and watched the police surge up the hill. Drew's auburn hair was easily visible in their high-powered police lights. He was directly behind Chief Warren Dredger, a sign of respect for his colleague, no doubt. I wondered if Chief Dredger had asked Drew to stay in Wyldwood. If Liberty so easily wiped the minds of officers clean, Chief Dredger must have some significant gaps in the public record.

"Well, hello officers," Liberty said, dialing up the charm as they filed past her into the greenhouse. "There's a situation, as you can see. I came by to visit Maisie Gledhill and found her like this."

"You came by this late?" Chief Dredger said.

"It's barely ten," she said. "I had a cab drop me off on the way home from the airport. I've been visiting family down in Strathmore County. Chief Gillock's stomping grounds. It got too hot for me."

Drew stared at her with eyes that were pools of darkness. "And you were that eager to see Maisie tonight? Why not wait till morning... when you could actually see her?"

"As you know, young man, I've only recently come back from abroad and I'm catching up with old friends. Maisie and I go way back. I looked up to her when I was a girl." She stared at Maisie now. "I never thought I'd look down at her in quite this way."

Drew turned to me. "And you, Miss Brighton? Were you also

called upon to reconnect with Mrs. Gledhill tonight? I don't believe you were old friends."

"Janelle isn't old enough to be an old friend," Liberty said, smiling. "She came to pick me up, of course."

"Oh? Then where is her car?" His eyes were still on me. "That sedan is hard to miss. Elsa, right?"

"Good one, Big Red," Mr. Bixby said. "But don't get too smart or Liberty will try a different memory spell on you."

Cousin Liberty's eyes landed on my dog. Like all the Brighton women, her eyes were green, but in her case, they were as cold and sharp as rare diamonds. She lifted a warning finger and my dog cocked his head in what was probably a challenge.

"Stop it," I told the dog, silently. "I've got enough to worry about without you two taunting each other."

"Maisie likes people to park in the bush," Liberty told the police. "She had a lucrative business selling botanicals and decorative plants, but she liked to keep that quiet. In Wyldwood, everyone wants their privacy."

Officer James Barrow, the young, fair-haired man Renata used to babysit, stepped forward now. "Your story doesn't add up, ma'am. Obviously you and the younger Miss Brighton are in cahoots over something that left Maisie—"

"As compost," Mr. Bixby suggested, with a chuckle. Luckily only I could hear him. "I'd suggest you get young Jimmy to cool his jets before Liberty does something impulsive you might regret."

"Incapacitated," James finished.

"I don't like your use of the word 'cahoots,'" Liberty said, surpassing Mr. Bixby's imperiousness. "It's unbecoming of a junior officer of the law." She looked at Chief Dredger. "Warren, I remember you as a child. Do you like your recruits using words like 'cahoots' over a citizen's dead body?"

"Miss Brighton, let's not get sidetracked here," Chief Dredger said, signaling Jimmy to stand down. "Regardless of the word choice, I'd have to agree that it's very strange you, Miss Scott and the younger Miss Brighton happened to be in the neighborhood at this late hour shopping for plants. Unfortunately, it's not the first time we've found your cousin—"

"I prefer niece," Liberty said.

"Cousin is good with me," I said.

"—loitering over a dead body."

Ren finally spoke up. "Chief Dredger, Janelle was not loitering, nor lurking, nor any other disrespectful 'L' word. I alerted the police about Mrs. Gledhill promptly. I'm sure your investigation will reveal she had plenty of detractors."

"All of them starting with B for Brighton," Jimmy Barrow said, leaning around Chief Dredger. "Janelle's mom got into fisticuffs with Maisie at Sour Grapes."

"I remember you telling me that before, when you were incorrectly accusing me of something, Officer Barrow," I said. "Regardless, my mom is down south with Gran right now. I suggest you call to confirm."

"That still leaves two Brightons," Jimmy muttered, as the chief eased him back again.

"Enough of this foolishness," Liberty said, tucking her purse under one arm. "You can't just single out Brightons as the first suspect in any crime, Warren."

"There's Renata, too," Jimmy said. "Someone disabled the security system and she's a whiz with technology."

"Jimmy!" Ren shook her finger at him. "I got along well with Maisie. At least, until recently. She was getting a little more crusty."

"Renata, pipe down," Liberty said. "I think Chief Dredger knows he needs to show some hustle here."

He rolled his eyes. "I don't need you to tell me how to do my job, Miss Brighton the senior."

There was a chance Liberty may have subsided if he hadn't

tossed the word senior into the mix, but her tight grip on her purse told me she was growing short on patience.

Tension seized my stomach and squeezed. I didn't know her well but the first time we'd faced the police together she hadn't hesitated to hurl a memory spell at them.

"Cousin Liberty," I said, "we're all tired, but this will go faster if we cooperate with the police. They'll realize soon enough we had nothing to do with what happened to Maisie. Then they can pursue the killer and take him off Wyldwood's streets."

"It's not necessarily a 'him,'" Jimmy said. "You're always casting shade at Oscar Knight, and he's a good guy."

"Tell them about the evidence Bijou found over there," Mr. Bixby said. "That poodle's been hopping around like a circus clown trying to get your attention."

"No one said anything about Mr. Knight, Jimmy. We're on the town's Christmas committee together and I'd hate to lose him." I gestured to the spot where Bijou was still percolating like a jumping bean. "When you start investigating, you might find something of interest over there. Along with some paw prints."

"A knife, perhaps?" Liberty said. "It looks like she was stabbed."

Bijou came back to Ren's side. "Pretty sure I smell poison, too. Just a wee bit."

"The rangleroot clouds everything," Bixby said. "It's so pungent."

Jimmy Barrow came forward again. "How about you leave the investigating to the experts, Miss Brighton Senior?"

Liberty took a step toward him. "I really don't like your attitude, Officer Barrow. You are leaving me no choice but to—"

"Cousin Liberty, don't. Please."

She lifted her hand over her head and started to bring it down in the same slashing gesture she'd used when spelling the police a few weeks ago. I took in a gulp of air and then hiccupped suddenly and loudly.

Liberty's hand stopped at eye level. "Janelle? Are you all right?"

"It was just a hiccup," Bixby said. "Rude, but hardly worth interrupting a good spell."

Ren looked from Liberty to me and then back. She probably expected it would take something more dramatic than a hiccup to stop Liberty in her tracks.

Covering my mouth, I mumbled, "Excuse me. Nerves, I guess."

I hiccupped again, and then again.

"Stop," Mr. Bixby said. "I don't care to be jostled around. You're giving *me* gas."

"Sorry," I said. I made a move to set him down but he stopped me.

"Look around, Janelle. Notice something different?"

Behind us, a row of sunflowers had appeared. They were tall enough that I couldn't have missed them before. Especially when they were my favorite flower. "That's odd," I whispered.

"Wait for it," he said. "And *go!*"

I hiccupped pretty much on cue and the flowers shot up another foot. "Uh-oh."

"Uh-oh, what?" Drew said. "What's going on, Janelle?"

Holding my breath, I tried to relax my diaphragm. The compulsion to hiccup was almost overwhelming.

Liberty's hand landed on my shoulder. "Chief Gillock, you'll need to excuse us. Janelle's in shock, it seems, and there's a good chance she'll lose her dinner."

All the police stepped back at once. I wanted to protest but Bixby was urging me to stay quiet. "Two more hiccups and those sunflowers will bust clear through the roof. Do you want to rain glass down on Big Red?"

"I need to question all of you," Chief Dredger said.

"Of course, and we look forward to it," Liberty said. Then she whispered, "Harold, the gourds, please."

The Aussie circled and tipped a bushel basket of decorative

gourds, and they whirled into a little vortex of wind. One of them promptly pelted Jimmy Barrow in the buttocks. The young cop gasped and staggered. He stepped on another gourd and fell to his knees.

Liberty squeezed my shoulder and propelled me forward. Harold left the gourds spinning and went ahead of us to clear a path through the ranks of police officers.

"Bye, now," Liberty called back. "I'm sure Janelle's stomach will settle by morning."

Outside, I released another hiccup and a sunflower exploded from the earth beside the footpath. It grew a couple of feet and flowered in about 15 seconds.

"I suggest you get a handle on that fast," Mr. Bixby said. "If you don't, the seeds will attract vermin." His voice got a little dreamy. "On the other hand, keep up the good work."

CHAPTER NINE

"Just watch the lava lamp. That's what it's there for, isn't it?"

Propping myself up on one elbow, I glanced at Mr. Bixby. He was curled up on a blanket on a worn wicker chair in the corner of my childhood bedroom. I'd offered him any number of nice blankets but he preferred the one Gran crocheted for me before I was born.

Perhaps I wasn't the only sentimental one in this room.

"I enjoy creature comforts as much as the next dachshund, that's all," he said. "We're known for our discernment, and Bridie used quality yarn for this."

Some squares of the blanket featured full daisies, others partial daisies, and still others just petals. When I was a child, I didn't realize it represented all the choices ahead of me.

"He loves me, he loves me not," Bixby said, with his snarky chuckle.

"I was thinking of the 'w' word and all the possibilities it brings." I sighed and dropped onto the pillow again. "And the others it chokes off."

The dog unfurled and rolled onto his belly, short legs

outstretched. "I've always enjoyed a good philosophical discussion at three a.m. But then, I don't need or desire much sleep anymore."

"Maybe we'll put a pause on that. I still need sleep like a normal person."

"Normal people don't sneeze flowers into existence," he said. "Although sunflowers have petals like the daisies, too. Don't think it escaped my notice that Drew sent you sunflowers for your launch. And now you're creating your own out of thin air."

I covered my face with the other pillow and mumbled, "It was a hiccup, not a sneeze. And it's never happened before."

"Imagine what you could do with a sneeze. More force behind it."

The pillow muffled my groan. "Must have been a buildup of stress. It's just one thing after the other. Liberty pushed me over the edge."

"I'd put the blame on her, most certainly. But I don't think it's just stress. You've been in much more complicated situations and kept your romantic fantasies grounded."

I propped myself up again and stared at him. "What do you mean?"

He rolled onto his side and sighed. "Must I spell everything out? Liberty said she gained magic from you and left something behind. I'd say you got the short end of the hiccup."

"You think this is something she passed on?"

"Didn't you notice her reaction? She couldn't get out of the greenhouse fast enough."

"I thought she was just being nice."

"I think she understood the implications of magical hiccups, possibly because she has experienced them herself." He examined one chunky paw. "Remember, this never happened before you healed her and you've said you haven't felt wholly yourself since that night."

Now I sat up in bed. "Seriously? She gets a share in my psychic powers and I get the hiccups? How is that fair?"

He chuckled and sat up, too. "If life were fair I'd have long legs and I wouldn't have died prematurely." After a moment, he added, "On the other hand, if life were fair, others may have earned another turn on this planet before I did. I'm not sure why I won the lottery and came back as your dog."

Hugging my knees, I smiled at him. "We both won the lottery. I couldn't do this without you."

"Oh, you could but you wouldn't have nearly as much fun." He watched as I swung my legs over the side of my twin bed. "We're giving up on sleep, are we?"

"Yeah. I'm worried about what happened to Maisie. Someone may have framed Liberty. And by someone, I mean Oscar. Since he couldn't kill her, he probably wants to put her out of commission in the regular way."

"No jail will hold Liberty," Bixby said, as I searched for my clothes in the light of the lava lamp. "I notice you're dressing like a vandal again, rather than a vixen storekeeper."

I slipped my arms into a black jacket and shoved the balaclava into my pocket. "Thought we'd go back to Maisie's greenhouse and take another look around."

He stuck his head under the crocheted blanket. "Nope. I am not thrashing through that bush again. Liberty had the right idea about that."

Liberty had told us to collect the car and pick her up on the road but she was gone by the time we got there. When I called, she said she was at home—specifically the manor she'd bought back from the Skinner family. I didn't believe her. She had sounded out of breath, for starters. Another thing she'd picked up in our energy transfer was my fitness level. For a woman technically in her seventies, who'd been on the brink of death a month ago, she was in good shape now. Private kickboxing and jujitsu instructors were seeing she made the most of it.

And all I got out of the bargain was a bad case of hiccups.

"All you *know* you got," Bixby said. "So far. I daresay there's more. Some of it might be interesting."

I put my hands on my hips. "Are you really going to loll around in crocheted daisies when you could be helping solve a mystery?"

Sighing, he pulled his head out of the yarn and stood up. "Having reminded myself of my luck in winning the life lottery, I suppose I'd better fulfill my duty. That begins by warning you Big Red will very likely still be at the crime scene."

I lifted him carefully and brought the blanket along for the ride. "I left your coat at the store, so maybe you should snuggle up in this."

He flailed in the daisies but I got him swaddled even as I tiptoed out of the house.

"I am not your dog-baby," he said. "I demand the use of my legs. Such as they are."

Setting him on the passenger seat, I loosened the blanket. "Your legs are exactly as they should be for a pedigreed dachshund. Your lip is another matter."

"I could say the same of you." He rose to stare out the window. "Where are we going? This isn't the route to Maisie's."

"There's more than one route to Maisie's," I said, driving into town. I found parking on a side street near the store. My usual place was available but I didn't like the idea of people knowing I was there at this hour.

"Maybe I'll just hang out here with the daisy blanket," he said. "Because I have this notion you're about to dive in way over your head."

I turned off the car and pulled out the key. "Maybe. But possibly not over Liberty's head. Let's find out if she left me anything more useful than hiccups."

The dog stepped onto the passenger seat to make it easier for me to pick him up. He wasn't planning to miss this show.

We slipped in through the back door, collected *Everyday Spells for Everyday Magic* from its hiding place, and then hit the road again. Without Ren to hack through the bushes, I decided to park much closer to Maisie's house and take our chances.

A quarter mile from our destination, I pulled off the road and into the bushes.

"You're just going to leave the old heap for Big Red to find? The sun will be up before long and Elsa is hard to miss."

"Only if she's visible," I said. "That's what we're working on today. If all goes as I hope."

"Which it never does," Mr. Bixby said. "I hate to be a Debbie downer, but someone has to play realist."

"You're not wrong," I said. "Things don't always go as I hope but they often go better than I fear. I guess it's all in how you frame it."

Pulling the spell book out of my bag, I set it on the trunk and then lifted the cover. As always, energy tingled in my hand as I ran my fingers over it and the pages came along for the ride.

I thought it might open to a spell I'd used a few times before to reveal things, but instead the pages stopped at an illustration of... nothing. It was the only spell I'd seen so far that featured only words.

"Liberty lost her creativity when she concocted this one," Bixby said, leaning out of my arms to take a look.

"Maybe that's the point," I said. "I'm looking to become like this blank page. Invisible."

"Why couldn't you just use the ox spell? It's worked before to get the car to disappear."

"By accident. As an unintended consequence. We want to be deliberate about this."

The spell's title was "Vanish into the Mist," which suited the occasion perfectly.

"Fog, mist, what's the difference?" Bixby said. "Oh right, precision is everything when it comes to magic."

I looked away from the book before reading the spell. Focus and deliberation were definitely part of the precision Bixby was talking about.

"Let's think this through first," I said. "I'll put the spell book in the trunk, say the spell, and it should vanish with the car. Then I'll say it again to vanish myself. You'll tell me if it worked. You'll become invisible yourself and we can both walk into the greenhouse unnoticed."

"Until you hiccup," he said.

"I won't hiccup. That was nerves."

He cocked his head skeptically. "And now you're completely calm?"

"Pretty much, because it's just the two of us. I get performance anxiety in front of Liberty. And Mom, for that matter."

"I don't think I've ever felt like that," he said. "But if I had, death would have killed it. Once you come back, you realize how silly most fears are."

"Makes sense. I wish I could just skip over the death part and be fearless now."

"Can't argue with that. The death part... well, enough said. We're staying upbeat. Positive. Spelling works better that way."

I carried the book around to the trunk and placed it carefully inside. Then I shone my phone light on the text. Normally, the script was ornate, even fanciful, but this time the lettering was plain. The spell itself was short and to the point, which I appreciated. There was so much information stuffed into my mind I needed a dog to hold the overflow.

Closing my eyes, I took a deep breath and imagined Elsa

vanishing from sight. Then I slowly spoke the spell aloud, enunciating every word carefully.

"Close," Mr. Bixby said, "but only half a cigar."

I opened my eyes. Elsa had vanished but the spell book appeared to be floating a few feet off the ground. Reaching out, I let my fingers connect with Elsa's side. I felt my way up the side of the trunk and closed it, hoping that would seal off the book from sight.

It worked! Elsa had created an invisible container for my spell book, which was quickly becoming my most prized possession after Bixby.

"May I always be number one," he said. "Now, vanish yourself and let's get on with this. When the sun comes up, it'll bring more cops. They may not see you, but they'll still be able to bump into you."

"True, good point. I'll need to stay out of the way."

Closing my eyes again, I pictured myself disappearing and repeated the spell.

When I opened them, I couldn't see my hands but the phone was hanging in the air. Now what? I didn't want to be without a phone in a situation like this.

The dog read my thoughts. "Try turning out the light and sticking the phone in your pocket."

I did as he asked, and he confirmed all was well. Then he vanished, too.

"How's this going to work? We'll smash into each other like bumper cars," I said. "What if I kick you by accident?"

There was a snort of canine disgust ahead of me. "Obviously I have an advantage here in that I can smell you. But if you care to use those psychic powers of yours, I bet you can get a good idea of where I am. In the meantime, enjoy listening to me issue commands."

I couldn't help laughing. "Who's the dog now?"

"Finally, we've got our roles sorted out. Miss Brighton... *heel.*"

CHAPTER TEN

B y the time we reached Maisie Gledhill's greenhouse there were only a few police officers on duty.

Unfortunately, two of them were Chiefs Dredger and Gillock. Jimmy Barrow was there, too, literally crawling on his hands and knees under the high-powered lights. Whatever evidence Bijou had noticed with her fine nose, Jimmy had likely found, too.

"It's still yours for the taking," Bixby said, using our internal line. "You don't have a dog's nose, but you have your ways."

"Works best if I can touch someone, though."

"Wouldn't that be so fun?" Bixby said, chuckling. "He's wearing gloves but his neck is bare. Just the lightest touch and—"

Jimmy Barrow let out a very shrill scream for a man and scrambled away from my fingers. He looked over his shoulder at the place where I had been standing, till I stepped aside.

"What's wrong, James?" Drew asked, staring around.

"I—I felt something touch my neck," the younger man said.

"Just the breeze," Drew said. "It's always so windy these days."

Jimmy grumbled under his breath. "Only if it's a tropical wind. That was warm."

Bixby chuckled again. "I wondered about that. Did you get anything?"

I nodded and realized he wouldn't see the movement.

"It's okay, I'm in your head, remember? I felt the nod."

"What a team," I whispered mentally.

"You don't need to whisper either," he said. "Being invisible has you rattled, which I understand. Felt the same way the first time and I'm still not used to it." He brushed against my leg and I jumped. "Just trying to be comforting. You know, like a regular dog."

I let out a shaky breath and Jimmy looked in my direction. He couldn't hear our conversation but huffing and puffing wouldn't get past him.

"The evidence?" Mr. Bixby pressed.

"Garden clippers," I said. "That's what Bijou found. They're over there."

We edged away from Jimmy to a folding table where several items sat in clear plastic bags. The clippers looked pretty much the same as the ones in our tool shed at home, although I couldn't pull out my phone to get a photo.

"Just crack the bags so I can take a whiff," Bixby said.

I did as he asked.

"Rangleroot," he said. "Bicksberry. Hemlock. A hint of olavia. And something else I don't recognize that could be the toxin Bijou detected. And on top of all that? Maisie's blood."

"So we have the murder weapon," I mused. "Anything to identify the killer?"

"No, but there's a lot going on here, even for a discerning nose."

"I suppose someone broke in to rummage around and then Maisie arrived. From what I could see, little had been disturbed until Harold got busy. She couldn't have put up much of a fight."

Bixby sniffed again, so delicately Jimmy wouldn't have heard it, though he was closer now. "The absence of DNA suggests a you-know-what."

"A 'w' word," I said.

"I've got a sanctioned 'w' word for you: walk. Let's take one." He was ahead of me now. "Jimmy's jittery, and as much as I enjoy that, it could lead to erratic behavior, such as punting an innocent dachshund."

"Not that innocent," I said, following him.

We moved around the greenhouse slowly, finding nothing else of particular interest.

"I *hear* something interesting," he said. "Listen with your good ear."

"My good ear?"

"The magic one," he said.

My feet stopped and when I tuned in mentally, I picked up raised voices. Two women were arguing somewhere outside the greenhouse.

"Let's go," I said, and we started moving again.

"Looks like we have a problem," Bixby said. "Our first big invisibility challenge."

The door had been propped open when we arrived, but Jimmy was dragging it closed.

We were stuck, and it wouldn't take a light touch to move it again.

"Just touch Jimmy and make a mental suggestion," Bixby said. "He might have a heart attack, but he deserves a shock for the way he treats Ren."

"Maybe I'll work through his jacket, since he felt the warmth of my fingers before."

Creeping up behind Jimmy, I waited till he was stooped and fully immersed in examining the ground underfoot. I ran a finger down his spine till I found a good spot to make my request. Then I gave him a little poke.

His squawk was so strident both chiefs jumped.

"What on earth, Jimmy?" Chief Dredger said. "Can you calm down?"

It was too late for that. Jimmy straightened and headed for the door. Pushing it open, he ran.

"And he vanished into the mist, just like the spell," Mr. Bixby said.

"I only wish we could have filmed it for Ren." I followed Jimmy quickly before the door closed again.

That's where I really slipped up. I was in such a hurry to get out that I didn't wait for my signal from Mr. Bixby.

My boot connected with the invisible dog and he let out a few doxy curses.

"Uh-oh." I stumbled and bumped into the doorframe.

"Quiet," the dog said. "Keep moving. And for the love of all that's pedigreed, don't—"

I hiccupped.

CHAPTER ELEVEN

M r. Bixby circled and snapped at my pant legs, managing to catch some fabric. "Hurry. But don't run because you'll—"

I fell.

Of course, I did.

Seeing the sunflowers spring up along the path made me so flustered it was no wonder I stumbled. I crawled around, deliberately crushing their thick stalks with my hands. These weren't ordinary sunflowers. They practically fought back. Wanting to be alive, it seemed, shouting their showy message.

"At Big Red, obviously. It's almost like you want to be caught. Luckily you're still invisible. Just get up and get going. Act like nothing happened."

I pushed myself to my feet and stomped the last two sunflowers before moving further away from the greenhouse. When I turned, however, Drew was framed in the doorway.

"Can he see them?" I swallowed a half-hiccup. "Bixby, one of the flowers is back up and growing."

"My eyes work just fine," he said. "Plus they're giving off a strange odor."

"Not magical flatulence! Please tell me it isn't that."

There was a strategic pause as he decided how far to play me. Likely he knew that I'd expose us if he had too much fun. "Not that. Nowhere near that foul. But look at Red. Sniffer's up."

I hoped it was one of Mr. Bixby's jokes, but Drew had indeed lifted his chin. He sniffed audibly and looked around. Luckily, the sunflowers—crushed and otherwise—were outside of the wide circle of light. Barely. In two hours, they'd be screaming for attention, because sunflowers didn't grow in Wyldwood in late November. At least, not *outside* a greenhouse.

"Hang tight," Bixby said. "Wait till Red goes back inside. Then you can set a little fire, like you did in Whimsy that day." After a second, he hastily added, "Only smaller. Much smaller."

Drew held out a good few minutes before finally retreating to join his colleague. After the door closed, I circled back and touched each of the sunflowers, extinguishing them like so many bright, toppled candles. I felt badly doing it.

"They're not children," Bixby said, his voice a little further away.

"They are, sort of. I grew those pretty babies and I felt a strange little tug when they died."

"You can grow more sunflowers anytime. All you need to do is drink a tin of soda too fast and it'll turn into a scene from the French countryside."

I followed him, with a last look of regret at my frizzled darlings. Picturing them, I whispered the invisibility spell and they vanished. "Why didn't I just do that instead? No reason to kill them."

"There was, though," he said. "I saw your original sunflower nearly drill through the roof at Whimsy. If these kept growing invisibly, your handsome chief might have broken his nose when he walked into them. Or worse."

An image of Drew doing just that popped into my mind, apparently at my dog's bidding. He laughed, but I shuddered.

"Come on," he said, his voice growing fainter in my head as he moved away. "We'll miss the show."

We very nearly did.

Ahead of us, someone who looked like a younger version of Maisie, only with a full head of salt and pepper hair, was following an older woman up the long driveway toward the garage. "Yeah, go," she said, shaking her finger. "My mother didn't allow you on this property, Sonia Dinogue, and you know it."

"I have every right to come over and ask the police what happened," Sonia said, turning so quickly Maisie's daughter nearly ran into her. "It's a matter of public safety. If your mother was murdered, Trina, who knows who might be next... Me? You?"

"Is that a threat?" Trina clutched a down parka closed over what appeared to be a nice dress. That's when I remembered the bridal shower. Had Maisie left the party to check out an intruder? "If it is, it's in very poor taste. I just lost my mother."

"As if I'd threaten you when the place is crawling with cops." Sonia thought about how that sounded and backtracked. "I'd never threaten you at all."

The older woman was wearing a parka, too, but hers topped pink flannel pajamas adorned with white ducks. On her feet were muddy, half-laced work boots.

"Why are you really here?" Trina asked. "You and Mom never got along."

"Unfortunately, your mom had run-ins with a lot of people. You took after your dad." Sonia smiled and it seemed like she was kinder than first impressions had suggested. "Poor man. She drove him to—"

"Miss Dinogue," Trina interrupted. "This really isn't the time for comments on either of my parents. I'm—"

"An orphan, now," Sonia interrupted in turn. "I understand. It's a terrible realization, but it happens to all of us if we live long enough. At least you had time together after you moved back home."

Trina blinked a few times, perhaps taking this in. It was true and even made me blink along with her. I'd barely reunited with Mom but I most certainly didn't want her gone.

Mr. Bixby poked me in the shin. "Plenty of time to ponder later. When we're both visible."

I wanted very much to pick him up, but even if I could find him, there was a real risk of one of us becoming visible and exposing the other.

Sonia cleared her throat and tried again. "All I wanted to know was what happened to your mom. For my own safety."

Trina managed to shake off the worst of her shock. "The decent thing to do would be to call the police station for information, rather than tromp all over Mom's grass. She cared about every blade on this property."

"It's November, Trina. The grass has passed away, too, at least till spring. At which point, I suppose you'll be the owner." She stuck out her hand. "How about we turn over a new leaf?"

Trina flinched back. "I'll never be friends with you, Miss Dinogue. Mom would roll over in her..."

"Greenhouse," Sonia supplied. "It's where she would have wanted to pass, Trina, and perhaps you'll find some comfort in that in the days to come. I've never known anyone with such a talent for growing as Maisie. She could make touchy tropical seeds spring to life. Her tiny greenhouses within greenhouses were nothing short of genius. Did you know someone was trying to get her to participate in a research project?"

The frown on Trina's face told me it cost her something to ask. "What research project?"

"Some botanical digest from Europe. The writer had an accent I didn't recognize. Came over to see if I could persuade Maisie to talk." A hint of scorn crept into her voice. "As if I could talk your mom into anything. She hated me before she knew me."

Crossing her arms, Trina shook her head. "Not before she knew you. It was only after she found you trespassing. She was a genius with plants and didn't want to share her trade secrets. I'm sure she said no to the researcher."

"No doubt. There's never much money in academics." Sonia took a couple of small steps forward. "I assume the traffic in and out of here brought the steady flow of dollar signs your mother wanted. All the movers and shakers in town passed through at one time or another. Perhaps it's just a coincidence that one of the biggest is back."

"Does she mean Liberty?" I whispered to Bixby. "Is she one of the biggest?"

"Guess so," he said. "Big enough that Oscar used up a lot of chits with his friends to take her down long ago."

"Mom had a green thumb. End of story," Trina said.

"End of her story, yes," Sonia said. "But not of her storied green-house. There will be competition to take it off your hands."

Trina held her palms up. "You've said quite enough. No matter how many times you argued with Mom, she deserves a moment of respect now. My daughter is inside crying her eyes out. Tonight was her bridal shower and now it will forever be associated with her grandmother's passing."

Sonia backed toward the garage. "I am sorry for Brianna. She seems like a nice girl, despite that louse you married. Wolfrey Peck. I wasn't surprised about his industrial accident."

Now Trina backed away, too. "Brianna has suffered a lot of loss. We both have."

"Look at the bright side," Sonia said. "There should be plenty left behind from Maisie to cover the wedding of Brianna's dreams."

A gasp slipped from Trina's mouth. "You really are as tactless as Mom said."

"Age does that to a person, I suppose. True of your mom, too." Sonia's expression showed a mere hint of remorse. "At the risk of sounding even more insensitive, did it occur to anyone that Maisie may simply have touched the wrong thing? Or consumed the wrong thing? That greenhouse was deadly, even for those in the know."

Mr. Bixby poked my shin again and murmured, "She's got a point. There were things in there I've never smelled before and they made my head ache. Generally, the more bitter a plant smells, the more bitter its impact."

Trina turned and walked up the stairs. "If I knew what happened, I wouldn't tell you, Miss Dinogue. Direct your nosiness to the police. Or get some farfetched tales from the rumor mill. I'm sure it'll be burning up tomorrow."

"No doubt." Sonia turned and shone a bright flashlight into the opening of a small trail in the bushes. "We can at least agree on that."

Trina stepped into the house and watched Sonia go from the other side of the screen door.

"Let's follow Sonia," I said. "Bet she doesn't go straight home. Someone's jonesing for the contents of Maisie's magical garden."

Bixby grunted agreement but then we both recoiled mentally in the same moment.

Snakes. The sense of dark magic coiling in my subconscious normally announced the arrival of Oscar Knight.

"Ugh. What's he doing here?" I asked, as the dog pressed me to stay in place. "Wherever he actually is."

"The same thing as Sonia, no doubt," Bixby said. "Maisie has some priceless botanical gems in her greenhouse and there's probably a stream of eager visitors lining up to get a cutting or two."

"But it doesn't sound like just anyone can grow these things. Maisie may have been cantankerous but she had talent."

"Hush now," the dog said. "Mr. Knight tends to rattle you. Deep, even breaths, my friend. I don't need to tell you what will happen if you—"

"I won't hiccup."

"Good, because I can feel him slithering out of the bushes close by."

Indeed, Oscar Knight's elegant profile stood out against the bushes not far from where Sonia had gone in. However, he was situated closer to the greenhouse.

He looked in our direction and for a terrifying moment, I worried he could see right through my "disguise." But perhaps he was simply checking the house. The door was closed now and there was no sign of Maisie's family in the windows.

Still, Oscar waited and the slight shift of his chin told me he was scanning for trouble. Bixby and I froze in position, trying to outwait him.

Finally, he stepped onto the path and moved swiftly and silently toward the greenhouse. A few yards from the door, he stopped suddenly and bent over. Plucking at something, he straightened and held it up for close inspection.

My sunflower. Or the frizzled remains of one I'd missed in my demolition.

"Do not add a fresh one to the bouquet," Mr. Bixby murmured in my head. He was likely quiet to avoid startling me into an unfortunate paroxysm.

Oscar pulled something out of his pocket. It rustled like a plastic bag. A doggie poop bag, I realized. Opening it, he dropped the remains of my sunflower inside and pocketed it.

"That can't be good," I said. "He's stealing my magical molecules. What can he do with them?"

"Honestly, I have no idea," Mr. Bixby said. "He wouldn't want to clone you, since you're already a thorn in his side."

An inner snake slithered, and at first I thought it was just a reaction to Oscar claiming anything that had belonged to me. But then I realized he was sending out sensory tendrils to try to find me. It wasn't surprising that he would know I was here. He had mentioned feeling nausea in my presence, just as I did in his, and invisibility might not shield that.

As if in confirmation, he came a couple of steps down the path and hissed, "I think I smell a Brighton. Come out where I can see you. We need to talk."

A cold chill ran down my spine. This man had tried to kill me twice already—that I knew of—and had very nearly succeeded in killing Liberty, who was far more powerful than I.

"More experienced," Bixby said. "Not necessarily more powerful. Though now that she filled up on your energy, she may well be your equal. You got the short end of that stick. And speaking of sticks..."

Oscar Knight had picked up a long stick and was sweeping it back and forth at waist level.

Sweeping for something solid, I presumed.

I started backing away even before Mr. Bixby pressed against my calves to get my feet moving.

"Go," the dog said, "and whatever you do, don't hiccup."

CHAPTER TWELVE

I successfully reversed the invisibility spell and drove back to Whimsy with a heavy foot. "Telling me not to hiccup is the surest way to get me to do just that, Bixby."

He chuckled from the passenger seat. "I beg to differ. Did you hiccup?"

"No, but it's all I could think about. There was no space left in my mind to figure out what Oscar was doing."

"The time to think about what Oscar is doing is never while he's sweeping for you with a dowsing rod. There's a time to advance and a time to retreat and get help from your cousin."

I turned onto Main Street and took my usual parking spot. The sun would rise soon and I was often there even earlier. "Did I leave the lights on? It's bright in there."

"Sinda?" he asked.

"She'd have gone straight downstairs, like always."

He lifted his nose to the crack in the window. "Don't smell a thing. Good or bad."

I left the car running while I reached out with my sensory tendrils. Were they any different from Oscar's snakes, when push came to shove?

"Yes," Bixby said. "Different and better. Do you think I'd have crossed back from perpetual peace for magical flatulence?"

"Well, he could detect me back there and we can detect nothing here. And yet someone is clearly in my store."

"Perhaps was. Past tense." He nosed my arm to get me moving. "Best to be on the alert, though."

"At least we know it isn't Oscar," I said, turning off the car. "He couldn't have beaten me here."

"Only a rocket could have," Bixby said, taking my seat as I left it so that I could grab him more easily.

I found the door to the store unlocked and stepped inside. The little bell overhead didn't give me its usual musical greeting. In fact, all I picked up was a tiny, tinny clink. Had someone disabled it? If so, it would be a shame as I'd grown fond of its trilling.

"Hello? Who's here?" My voice had a slight wobble. "Sinda?"

"And you call yourself a psychic?" There was a laugh from the back room that I might have found pleasant if it didn't grate on my nerves. "I could tell it was you half a mile away."

"Using stolen power," Mr. Bixby said. "Maybe you didn't leave Janelle enough juice, Liberty."

"She has plenty." Cousin Liberty stepped into the doorway looking a little worse for wear. Not as bad as when she was suffering from black magic, but nowhere near as polished as when she left Wyldwood to visit Mom. "Janelle needs to work on tapping into it. I've been training for weeks and it's growing like a weed. Right, Harold?"

The dog didn't bother answering before coming to greet me with a wiggle.

"Not the day to joke about weeds," I said. "We've just come from Maisie's greenhouse."

"So I gathered. And if I'm reading things correctly, you ran into my nemesis while there. Did he see you?"

"No, thank goodness. The invisibility spell from your book did the trick. But there was another sunflower incident."

Liberty turned away, running her fingers over the smooth counter. "It happened again? What's going on?"

"I was hoping you could tell me," I said. "This never happened before I helped you recover from Oscar's spell."

Bixby demanded to get down and strutted over to Liberty. "She saved your life, in case you've forgotten."

"I haven't forgotten and I've never denied it," she said. "There's no need to keep reminding me."

"Sure, there is," he said. "Because you left a bad case of magical hiccups behind and it could get Janelle killed."

"Harold," she said, "could you put that dog in his place? His sass annoys me."

The Aussie went back to sit by her side without doing a thing. He managed to show his loyalty to both of us without saying a word.

"Bixby, we don't know that's what's happening," I said. "Surely Cousin Liberty would have mentioned a problem like that."

Coming over to the counter, she rested her arms on it. Up close, she looked even more worn. "At my age, a sleepless night shows," she said, reading either my mind or my expression. "Enjoy youth while it lasts."

"Then why are you here instead of sleeping off the excitement?"

"Because I wanted to discuss what happened," she said.

"And...?" Harold prompted.

"And I wanted to apologize about the hiccups. I assume you did pick up that problem when you helped me."

"You have magical hiccups? Is it a chronic condition?"

"Heavens, no. I outgrew them eons ago and you will, too. It was just a nervous tic back when I was a novice." She was grinning when she turned to face me. "Got me into no end of trouble at school. That's why my mother pulled me out and educated me herself. In my case, it wasn't just sunflowers that exploded."

Bixby motioned for me to lift him onto the counter. "Tell us more."

"I'd rather not. Nor do I like a dog to be elevated beyond his station." She flicked her fingers at him as he faced her from closer range. "This one already has delusions of grandeur."

"Harold sits on stools and towers over me, and I don't mind at all," I said. "Can we go back to the hiccups? It sounds like you transferred a case of beginner's nerves to me. How did you get over it?"

"Time and practice, like anything else. If it's just sunflowers, consider yourself lucky."

"It stopped being lucky when one of them landed in Oscar's pocket," I said. "What could he do with it?"

Her green eyes showed a hint of alarm. "Oscar took a sunflower?"

"The charred remains. I had burned the evidence but apparently it was still of interest."

"What was he even doing there?" Liberty started pacing and Harold followed close behind. "Or was he there before I even arrived?"

"No idea. Do you think he might have killed Maisie?"

"He's capable, obviously, but I doubt it. Maisie's green thumb was too useful. She'd take on any project for a price. There are others who can grow, but no one had her infrastructure and flair. I daresay Oscar used her fine botanicals to take me down. Now he'll need to find an alternate vendor." Reaching up, she touched the bell and it gave a little chirp that sounded cautiously optimistic. "Maisie's passing leaves an opening in the market for an aspiring gardener."

"I wondered about that," I said. "I overheard Maisie's daughter arguing with Sonia Dinogue, the neighbor. Sonia said someone was interested in studying Maisie's work. Someone with an accent."

Liberty made a short turn in front of the counter and strode back to the door. "I'm sure Maisie had no interest in giving away her trade secrets. She had the market cornered. Why empower competition?"

I ran my hand along Bixby's back just as the phone rang. "Uh-oh. Mom never calls this early."

Liberty, normally so bold, let Harold escort her into the back room. "Tell her I said hello."

"Tell her yourself," I said, putting the phone on speaker. "Hey, Mom. Liberty and I are just putting our heads together at Whimsy."

"Oh, I know," Mom said. "I heard from one of my local operatives. Meanwhile, your gran and I have just been putting *our* heads together and trying to figure out how to get you out of this mess." There was a quiet discussion on their end and then Mom added, "We blame Liberty, of course."

"Me?" Liberty sounded like the beleaguered schoolgirl of long ago. "I didn't do anything."

"The rumor mill says you were caught standing over Maisie Gledhill in her greenhouse last night," Mom said. "You must have made good time home from here."

Liberty slipped past Harold and took up the gauntlet Mom had thrown down. "Does the rumor mill say I found your daughter at the site?"

"I found *you*, technically speaking," I said. "Although there's no point quibbling when we were both caught at the scene of a murder. This would go better if we worked as a team, Cousin Liberty."

"I don't do teams." She resumed pacing. "In my day, it was every woman for herself."

"You're the Brighton matriarch," Gran said, now on speaker. "We're very much a team."

"There was no team when I vanished, Bridie," Liberty said. "You were all just as happy to think I was dead."

Bixby snapped at Liberty's sleeve on the next pass. "I call red herring on that. The point is, we found you standing over Maisie. And you've left Janelle with a bad case of magical hiccups."

The squawk of horror came from Mom, who quickly enlightened Gran about what the dog had said.

"No, Libby! Not magical hiccups!" Gran sounded horrified. "You killed the school nurse that way."

"Nonsense." Liberty glared at the phone. "She was startled and fell awkwardly, that's all."

"On her own hypodermic," Gran added. "Oh, how people talked."

"It was a freak accident," Liberty muttered, retreating again. "Doesn't pay to startle a young witch."

"Marvelous," Mr. Bixby said. "Your hiccup ended in a fatality. It's good for Janelle to know what she's up against."

Liberty was in the back room now but she stuck her head out. "She'll outgrow it, just like I did."

"Outgrow it?" I said. "By when?"

"Quite quickly, if you apply some confidence to the situation. I've become familiar with the powers you're packing, Janelle, because I'm packing them, too. You should feel supremely confident."

"Just like you're supremely confident?" Bixby countered. "You're hiding from Bridie."

Liberty strutted out of the back room. "I'm not afraid of anyone, and especially not Bridie. Shelley's another matter."

"It's wise to be cautious when you've engaged a mother's wrath," Mom said. "I'm incensed that you've left my daughter more vulnerable than ever before. I'll be on the next flight home."

"There's nothing you can do about magical hiccups," Liberty said. "You know that, Shelley. Besides, all it's done so far is cause your daughter to grow spontaneous sunflowers."

"Sunflowers?" Mom asked. "Why sunflowers?" Gran quietly

enlightened her, causing Mom to cluck in disgust. "This is no time for romance. It will only lead to trouble."

"When has that ever stopped a Brighton lady?" Gran said. "Unlike Janelle, the rest of us have a bad picker."

Liberty sniffed. "Who says Chief Gillock is a good pick? There's something funny about him. My memory spell barely stuck."

"How about we stick to the problem at hand?" I said. "Maisie Gledhill is dead and Liberty was caught on the scene."

"As was Janelle," Liberty added quickly. We sounded like bickering kids.

"Good thing I'm out of town," Mom said. "I'd be a suspect, too, since Maisie and I had words."

"Fisticuffs in a saloon, as I understand it," Liberty said. "But Maisie made plenty of enemies. The only question is who got to her first."

I shared everything I knew about what happened to Maisie with Mom, Gran and Liberty, with frequent interjections from Mr. Bixby that Mom translated for Gran.

When I was finished everyone stared at me. I couldn't see Mom and Gran doing so but I felt the weight of their concern.

Liberty's expression was inscrutable. "So Oscar Knight sensed you were there and you managed to stay invisible?" she asked.

"Not a single hiccup," Bixby said. "I was proud of her."

"She's learning already," Liberty said. "You see, Shelley? She'll be fine."

After some muttering on the other end, Gran spoke up. "There's only one thing to do: keep a low profile and let the police handle this."

Liberty caught my eye and held her finger to her lips. "Agreed. We need to back right off. As family matriarch, I'll set Janelle a good example, you can be sure of that."

Mom wasn't falling for it. I could feel her mental gears turning.

"What else did you give her in your energy transfer, Liberty? I assume you disgorged everything like a bloated tick."

Harold growled and I didn't blame him. It was a horrible comparison.

Gran muttered again on her end before speaking up. "You were very good at disappearing at the first sign of trouble, Liberty. Did you pass that to my granddaughter?"

Liberty grinned. "Actually, it doesn't seem like she got that gift from me. She tends to run *toward* trouble."

"Janelle," Mom said. "There's something you're not telling me. I can feel it. What else is going on?"

"There's a little situation," I said. "At the Beanstalk Café. A new ghost dog."

"Not another one," Gran said. "I love dogs but yours seem to come with a whole lot of trouble."

"I object," Bixby said. "And I object for Harold, since he won't bother."

I took a deep breath. "Not only that... Oscar's wife met me there and asked for my help. More specifically, some help with her dog."

Everyone stayed quiet as Mom digested the news. "Octavia Knight's gone behind her husband's back to get your help?"

"Yeah. Tavi is on the outs with Oscar over what he did to Harold and wants to cast a protective spell over her ridgeback. It requires rangleroot, which is why I was at Maisie's."

I pulled the printout of the spell from my purse and sent a photo of it to Mom. Liberty reviewed it at the same time.

"Looks legit," Liberty said. "I have something similar I already used on Harold."

"It could be a trap," Mom said. "Janelle, you cannot come between a man and his wife."

"That's exactly what Oscar said at Whimsy's launch," I said. "But I can't *not* help a woman with her dog, Mom. That's what I'm on the planet to do."

"You're supposedly here to rescue *ghost* dogs," Mom said. "Octavia's ridgeback is very much alive."

"Philomena is a good dog, and I understand why Tavi is worried. She thinks Liberty might come after the dog in retaliation for what Oscar did."

"As if I could ever hurt a dog," Liberty said. "But I suppose others might, if they felt it could harm Oscar through Tavi."

Mom was pacing at her end. Her heels had rubber tips but I could hear the thuds on Gran's tiled floor. I'd paced in that kitchen myself. "If you must insert yourself between the Knights, might I suggest you do so after Maisie's murder is solved?"

"That sounds reasonable," Liberty said. "If Chief Gillock is such a good pick, I'm sure he'll get things sorted out quickly."

I stared at Liberty. "If you gave me the rangleroot you stole from Maisie, I could share it with Tavi and wash my hands of it."

Liberty cocked her head. "How would you know about that?"

Harold joined the conversation for the first time. "I told you. Little guy has a good sniffer."

Mr. Bixby inclined his head modestly. "I used to forage for medicinal plants in my previous life. I haven't forgotten the basics."

"Rangleroot isn't a basic," Liberty said. "It's hard to come by and Maisie is one of the very few in hill country to cajole it along."

"Who else?" I asked. "Because it seems to be a hot commodity."

Liberty sighed. "I can't tell you for fear of activating your mother's wrath. Suffice to say I'll try to get my hands on a little more. Mine is already spent."

"Perhaps you could pass the rangleroot directly to Tavi and get Janny out of the middleman role," Mom said. "You're the one who got her there."

I expected Liberty to protest, but she didn't. Instead, she unlocked the front door, released Harold into the street, and called back, "I'll do what I can for the clan."

"And you, Janny?" Mom asked, after the door closed behind Liberty.

"I'm glad Liberty's on the case," I said, sidestepping the question. "I'm going down to the Beanstalk for a coffee. I'll mull over this hiccupping situation."

"Do be very careful with that problem," Mom said. "The school nurse wasn't the only victim. There was—"

Gran interrupted her. "No need to bog her down with detail, Shelley. Back in our day there were some bullies who picked on Liberty."

"Is Bridie saying they got what they deserved?" Mr. Bixby asked.

"No one deserves mushrooms growing out of their—" Mom stopped herself. "Never mind. It's bad enough I have to picture it."

"I can't wait to swap stories," Mr. Bixby said. "I have some good ones, too."

Mom hung up in disgust and Mr. Bixby chuckled. "She has it too easy with Sir Windbag. Time to see how a proper familiar operates."

CHAPTER THIRTEEN

V alerie Fairchild brightened as I walked into the Beanstalk with the dachshund under my arm. "It's so good to see you," she called, waving to my favorite table. "I'll bring over your coffee."

I thanked her and said good morning to the old man in the trench coat and fedora. He had beaten me there, although the café had likely only been open a few minutes. Looking up at me with a blank expression, he didn't answer, making me wonder if he spoke English. I settled on a smile and a wave before heading for my seat.

Atticus was far more emotive, fanning his gorgeous feathery tail. It was unmarked with freckles and waved a white flag in the already bright café. I loved how the sun was streaming in the windows from the eastern exposure. It helped chase away some of the bad memories associated with the place.

The friendly ghost setter grabbed my attention again by knocking a book off the shelf. Getting up to collect it, I saw it was Dickens' *David Copperfield*. There were a couple of his books on the shelf but Gran and I had never tackled them because of the length. It would have taken more milkshakes to get through them than she was willing to allow.

Setting the book back in its place, I reorganized some of the others into alphabetical order. It wasn't the first time. I'd always liked to see these books properly arranged. It was a matter of respect —to the authors, not Mitzy Lennox, who had seemed indifferent to the library.

"How about you leave those alone, buddy?" I whispered. "You're getting Valerie a little rattled and she seems like a nice lady. Am I right?"

His tail waved some more, as if in confirmation, but then he looked over at the old man. I turned just in time to see his fedora angle quickly away. Apparently he'd heard me talking to thin air.

"It happens," Bixby said. "If he's rude enough not to say good morning, I wouldn't worry about his opinion."

Sighing, I sat down, just in time to receive a very welcome cup of java. "Join me for a moment, Valerie. Has your—uh—problem continued today?"

Pulling out the chair opposite me, she sank into it heavily. "Every time I come around to wipe the tables there are books on the floor. Unless Wyldwood is subject to earthquakes, I'd say I have a problem. Plus, last night after I locked up, I could swear I heard howling inside."

I glanced at Atticus and his tail drooped. Someone apparently didn't enjoy being left behind.

"Interesting," I said, adjusting Mr. Bixby in my lap. "Thank you for letting me bring my dog in here. Are you a dog lover, too?"

For the first time, her smile seemed genuine. "Oh, yes. We always had a dog growing up. My mom was very fond of German shepherds."

"Never an English setter?" I asked. "It's a stunning breed."

She pursed her lips, pondering. "Don't believe I've ever seen one of those. Are they friendly?"

"Very much so, and quite large."

"I'd love to see one. When I worked in offices I didn't want to leave a dog alone so much. But I was hoping I might make it work here in Wyldwood. I'd just feel so much safer." Her fingertips drummed the table. "Not a German shepherd, though. They're good protection but too much dog for me at my age."

"I know what you're thinking, Janelle," Mr. Bixby said. "If a German shepherd is too much, you think a ghost dog won't be?"

I gave him a little tap to simmer down. "He's got a lot to say," I told Valerie. "Gets quite loud sometimes."

"I noticed, and it's delightful. I couldn't help wishing for one of my own after I saw you together yesterday."

"On the other hand," Bixby said, "maybe I misspoke. She seems nice."

Reaching across the table, I lightly touched Valerie's wrist-watch. In a world where people relied on phones to see the time, it was nice that the older generation still liked a watch. It was always easier to take a peek into someone's mind when there was jewelry. Preferably something with a stone, but anything worn often could help. "We appreciate the warm welcome you've given us. Especially when there's been a bit of gossip."

Images arose in her mind at the word and I saw she'd been fully briefed, mostly by Matilda Wentwhistle, the stylist at A Cut Above, where she'd had a trim upon arriving in town. Nodding, Valerie said, "People say things, but you learn to sort fiction from fact pretty quickly. If there's any question, you await confirmation. It always comes."

"A good attitude," Bixby said. "Shared by so few."

Still touching Valerie's watch, I brought up the latest news. "I suppose you've heard Maisie Gledhill died last night."

Now her eyes clouded with concern. "I was sorry to hear it. Especially when she bought my cupcakes for the bridal shower. The police are testing them for poison."

"Heart rate accelerating," Bixby said. "Rapid breathing. For what it's worth."

"Being part of any police investigation is always nerve-racking, Valerie. I should know, as I've experienced it firsthand."

She looked down at my fingers and moved her wrist away. "And will again, I suppose. Matilda Wentwhistle and Becca Mathews were waiting outside when I opened and they told me you and your aunt are suspects."

"Cousin," I corrected. "But they'll find out soon enough that we had nothing to do with it. Everyone slings mud at a time like this. I'm sure you'll hear of more suspects before the day is through."

"Already have," she said. "Apparently a friend of Mr. Knight's has a greenhouse operation and is looking to expand. But Maisie wasn't selling."

"Becca and Matilda told you that?"

She nodded. "I don't recall his name. Arnold something-or-other."

I let my fingers brush her watch again. Arnold Blatchford. I had never met him, but knew he was one of the quiet elite of Wyldwood Springs. In any other town, he'd be Oscar's golf crony. For all I knew, warlocks did golf.

"Situations like this aren't uncommon around here, unfortunately, Valerie. Are you sorry you took a chance on running this café in Wyldwood?"

Her head swept from side to side more quickly than I expected. "You know I had second thoughts yesterday, and you'd think after what happened with Maisie—one of my first customers—I would have regrets. But oddly enough, after you and your friends came over, I felt very differently about my decision. It's like you're my good luck charm."

I laughed. "Few people would consider me that, but it's very kind. This is going to sound strange, given what happened here, but I think this place is getting a new lease on life." I glanced over and saw Atticus wagging harder than ever. "Make that a leash on life.

You're going to need a dog, Valerie, and I bet I can find just the right one for you. I've rescued a handful now."

"I rescued you, as I recall," Mr. Bixby said, but his voice had less of an edge than usual.

"The right dog and person tend to rescue each other," I continued. "In the meantime, just keep your head down and the coffee flowing."

I picked up my cup to chug the dark brew. It was very good coffee, but after the night I'd had, anything would taste good.

"Are you leaving so soon?" She sighed as I slipped the straps of my bag up my shoulder.

"I need to run a couple of errands before the store opens," I said. It had been wise to set my regular hours later than most retail stores. I needed more flexibility than many.

The bell tinkled over the door. It was just a regular bell but I was glad Valerie had already replaced Mitzy's strident buzzer. I'd always theorized the former owner had kept it to deter people from staying too long.

"On the other hand," I said, "it looks like I'll have a word with a friend, first."

"Friend" was vastly overstating my relationship with Octavia Knight, but meeting twice in two days suggested more than mere acquaintanceship.

She had dressed once again as a screen siren, with a different designer scarf on her head, even bigger sunglasses, and a black wool jacket. I glanced over at the old man to see if he'd noticed her come in, but he appeared to be doing the crossword puzzle in the newspaper.

"In pen," Bixby pointed out. "The guy has confidence."

Valerie faded away discreetly and Atticus' tail picked up speed as the women crossed paths. He was a genial dog, that much was clear. So far, his only flaw was liking to toss the library around.

"That won't be the end of it," Bixby said. "As much as I like to disparage my competition, none of your so-called rescues is stupid. Even the poodle, silly as she is."

There was no time for debate as Octavia had already slid into the seat Valerie had occupied.

"Did you get it?" she asked. "The rangleroot?"

Mr. Bixby stared at her across the table. "No time for pleasantries?"

I followed Octavia's lead and got right to the point. "I'm sure you heard what happened. When we arrived, we found Maisie dead in her greenhouse."

"Under Liberty's boot, from what I heard."

"A lie," Bixby said. "I happened to be on boot level."

"Cousin Liberty didn't kill Maisie, Mrs. Knight." The allegation made me revert to her formal title. "She stopped by on her way home to collect some medicinal herbs. I assume that's what your husband was doing there as well."

"My husband?" Her sunglasses slid down her nose. "Oscar was there?"

I nodded. "I saw him strolling around while the police were investigating."

"So he didn't kill Maisie."

"No idea. But I suppose he wouldn't stick around if he had. He was heading to the greenhouse when I left. Maybe he wanted to speak to the police."

Her fingers splayed on the table and they looked bare without her rings. Pulling them out of a pocket in my purse, I slid them toward her. "I can't keep these, Mrs. Knight. By rights, they should go to Jared's wife, or his daughter if he has one." I tried to repress a shudder at the thought of him reproducing. "These are family heirlooms."

"Please keep them. I'll never wear them again."

I touched her wrist gently, finding a watch through the sleeve of her coat. "You can't be sure of that. All couples go through rough patches."

"Not like this. It's like I don't even know my husband. This morning I woke up and saw him creeping into the pool house and he looked like a stranger."

"When I worked at resorts, I heard so many stories of couples coming through tough times even stronger. I'm quite sure Oscar cares for you. It was obvious that day in my store."

She touched the wedding ring and spun it around. "He did when we were newlyweds. I have no doubt of that. Every single morning he brought me a cup of tea in bed." Picking up the ring, she inspected it closely. "Still leaves me tea in a thermos. Not today, however. I thought perhaps he'd had a..." Her voice drifted off.

"That sounds very romantic," I said, wishing I had more coffee. "He didn't have a date, if that's what you're wondering. On the contrary."

"On the contrary. Indeed. He was at the site of a murder. Just as he tried to kill Liberty, and worse, her dog."

She slid the rings back to me and I left them sitting on the table. "Mrs. Knight, we all know there are old grudges in this town. I will never forgive your husband for what he did to Liberty, but I doubt the Brightons have always behaved impeccably either."

"Liberty killed people," Octavia said. "Or so I've heard."

"Perhaps. The point is, we want the feud between our families to end here. With us. Right?"

Shoving the glasses back up her nose, she nodded. "But I still want to protect Philomena. Do you know of another source of rangleroot?"

I thought about asking her for more information on Oscar's crony, Arnold Blatchford, but it didn't seem wise to plant the seed. I wouldn't put it past Tavi to break into Arnold's greenhouse, and a fight between these powerful men would raise a lot of feathers in town.

"Not yet," I said. "Give me a little time. We both want our dogs safe and protected."

Adjusting her scarf, she gave a quick nod. "Keep the rings, Janelle. If I ever have that granddaughter, I'll know where to come."

I slipped them back in the pocket of my purse. "I hope you get that little girl one day."

"If Jared ever visits, I intend to set you two up. You're becoming like a daughter to me."

"Oof," Bixby said, as Octavia left. "Talk about looking a gift witch in the mouth."

Tucking him under my arm, I got up and headed for the door. "If you're taking a free pass on that word, Bixby, you'd better get ready... because I'm going to fire a wiener at you."

Unfortunately, I said the last words out loud as we passed the old man doing his crossword puzzle. He looked up, eyes wide under the fedora. Then he ducked.

Mr. Bixby laughed harder than he ever had, while Atticus frolicked beside the shelves knocking books around in a most undignified way.

I forced a smile onto my face, lifted my chin and strutted out.

Sometimes, all I could do was pull out the Brighton genes and fake it.

CHAPTER FOURTEEN

Renata was waiting for me on the window seat inside Whimsy. A large plastic container filled with three kinds of fancy pastries I couldn't name sat beside her.

"Wow, we're going upscale today," I said. "Is this your murder special?"

She gave me a sheepish grin. "Not exactly, but sort of. I figured you might want to visit Maisie's family and wouldn't want to arrive empty-handed. Based on what you texted, some sugar might help."

It never hurt, in my opinion, but I still had to turn down the sample she offered from a smaller tin. "My stomach's a little testy and I don't want to give it any excuse for a hiccup."

Getting up, she joined me at the counter. "It happened again?"

"Oh, yes," Mr. Bixby said. "Right outside the greenhouse."

Ren gasped. "Did Drew witness it? Or Jimmy Barrow?"

I took my time hoisting Bixby onto the counter. He was less likely to deliver wisecracks while dangling in mid-air, I'd found—a fact he confirmed by grumbling and pretending to snap at my wrist.

"No one saw the sunflowers," I said, setting him on the counter. "And I threw out the ones Drew gave me, to try to erase them from my memory."

"They were deader than Maisie anyway," Bixby said, giving his coat a few licks to settle his ruffled fur. "But you'll never forget them. Sunflowers are forever associated with your handsome chief."

"True. Because I never told him they were my favorites. No one ever chooses them, which is partially why I did. They're the most cheerful lonely flower in any garden."

The dog stopped licking to stare at me. "Are we going to wax poetic or tell Ren what really happened?"

I briefed her about seeing Oscar Knight on the Gledhill property and about Cousin Liberty admitting to her nervous habit of old.

"What a terrible thing to pass on to family," Ren said. "Did you get anything good in this mingling of powers?"

Mingling. What a strange word for what had happened, yet oddly appropriate. "Nothing she's told me about. There's a chance my powers will backfire on her as well."

Bixby gave a haughty sniff. "She's too arrogant to admit it, so we'll never know."

"Probably not." I zipped my coat again, wishing I had time to go home and change before our next visit. Casual dress code didn't fly with me, outside of hardcore sleuthing. "I'll just worry about reining in my spontaneous eruptions."

"Guess it could be worse than sunflowers," Ren said, picking up the larger container and letting Bijou lead her to the door. "Far worse."

"We'll see about that," Mr. Bixby said. "Oscar is probably having his sample analyzed now. Hard to say what he'll do with it. As you'll recall, Janelle, someone tried to use your hair and belongings to cast an extermination spell. I would think a flower straight out of your heart could be pretty potent."

I wanted to argue but feared he was right. "We'll just have to outwit Oscar again. Float like a butterfly, sting like a bee."

He permitted himself a chuckle as I lifted him down more gently. "That analogy works. The boxing champ, right?"

"Right," I said, walking out the door and then locking it behind us. "Let's try to interview both Trina Peck and Sonia Dinogue before eleven. If the store doesn't open on time it'll just give people more to talk about."

For the first part of the drive, the only sound was a somewhat suspicious clanking under Elsa's hood. I'd taken her to the mechanic for a thorough once-over after a spelling mishap weeks ago, but the guy hadn't appreciated her worth. Some mechanics just got it and some didn't. But he was the only show in town, so I'd have to explore options beyond Wyldwood's borders.

"Ethan's grand opening for the bistro is tomorrow night," Ren said, at last. "Do you think the police will allow it?"

I knew how much Ren was looking forward to the event. Ethan Bogart, the town's finest chef, had vacated the space where Flour Girl now bloomed to start a bigger restaurant. The two helped each other out quite often and it seemed like the spark was mutual.

"Hopefully. Ethan deserves a proper launch." I made a left turn, happy to be taking the main road instead of bushwhacking into Maisie's greenhouse. "Wouldn't be surprised if Drew comes to keep an eye on things."

"Including you," Bixby said, stretching out as much as he could on Ren's lap. Shoving Bijou off prime real estate was one of his great joys in life. "More as a suspect than a conquest."

"Leave Witchy alone," Bijou said, shoving him right back. "You'll make her belch more flowers."

"Bijou!" Ren sounded horrified. "Janelle does not belch."

Bixby laughed. "Belching is one of the great pleasures of living, as you'll find out one day. When you can't do it anymore."

I rolled my eyes. "I can think of many things I'd miss more. Like Ren's baking. Or a good cup of coffee." Patting the steering wheel, I added, "Or a nice drive with Elsa."

My dog flipped onto his back and pressed Bijou into the door.

"You do realize that a belch is just another name for a hiccup. It's one of many wonderful, natural processes."

"Just stop, Bixby." I pulled up to the curb near Maisie's driveway. "If there's any mention of natural processes here I'll end up having an outburst of some sort."

"Laughing is perfectly natural, too," he said. "Just saying."

"And highly inappropriate with a family that's just lost its matriarch. Whatever we thought of Maisie, they loved her."

Mr. Bixby turned back onto his stomach. "You don't know that. Always best to ditch your assumptions before investigating, is it not? Let your fingers do the listening."

I turned off the engine and nodded. "You're annoying but not wrong. We go in with open minds."

"Mine's always wide open," Bijou said. "Try to keep it mostly empty. Saves trouble."

"Not for us," Bixby said. "In fact, your inanities cause no end of suffering."

Ren grinned as she extricated Mr. Bixby from fluffy orange paws and handed him over to me. "What a pair. They've kicked my stomach till it hurts."

Taking my dog, I got out of the car. "We're a team, remember?"

I held onto Mr. Bixby because I didn't trust him to play nice on the ground. His grumbles confirmed it as Bijou trotted at the end of her lead. Ren tried to keep up while holding her baked goods steady.

"No sign of police cars," I whispered as we walked up the driveway and then climbed the stairs to the front porch. "They must have finished investigating here."

"That's a relief," Ren said. "I don't do my best work when Jimmy Barrow is trying to implicate me in every murder in town." Shaking back her shiny hair, she sighed. "How is it that there are so many murders lately?"

"You have to ask?" Bixby said. "They ramped up with Janelle's homecoming."

"What is that supposed to mean?" I adjusted him to rest on my hip so that one hand was free and then pressed the doorbell. "I was just living my life when all this started."

"On the contrary. You were running for your life... and then you stopped. That's when people started dying." He squirmed a little till he found a more comfortable position. "You turned to look trouble squarely in the face. As you should."

The face that peered out when the door opened certainly looked like trouble. Trina Peck, Maisie's daughter, glowered at us— or more specifically, at me. "What do you want, Janelle Brighton? You and your crazy mother and crazier cousin are not welcome on this property." She turned to Ren. "You either, Renata."

Summoning my most compassionate smile, I dove into dangerous water. "Trina, I don't blame you for feeling that way after what's happened, really I don't. In fact, I came to apologize for contributing to your stress in this difficult time. My family had nothing to do with Maisie's passing, but—"

"Don't even," Trina said. "You were found standing around her body. I don't know why you're not already sitting in the slammer. Maybe what people say about you and that visiting chief is true."

"Don't ask," Mr. Bixby said, now on our internal line. "It's a red herring, and I'm rather an expert on those."

"We were here looking for your mom," I said. "Trying to buy some of the medicinal plants she grew so well. She was the premier gardener in Wyldwood Springs."

"True, and she didn't want to sell to the Brightons," Trina said. "This town is run on alliances, and my mom made a deliberate decision not to deal with your family."

"A fact that left us high and dry in some situations," I said. "She was the only source of certain necessary plants."

Trina shrugged. "Not my problem you people can't source the things you need. Although you made it her problem, didn't you?"

Stepping forward, Renata flashed her brilliant smile and held out the container of fancy pastries. "I'm sure your family is gathering and will be hungry. I baked something special for you."

A quick shake of the head repelled Ren's gesture. "We don't want your guilt gifts. Just go."

Ren popped the lid and released the most delectable aroma. "Your mom was such a fan of my baked goods when I worked at the Beanstalk Café. She served them at family parties."

Perhaps the smell tapped into nostalgia, because Trina's head bobbed. "She did talk about your cakes. There was one in particular."

"Strawberry mousse cake," Ren said, pointing at one of the treats in the container. "This Danish is a variation on that. In honor of your mom. I hope you'll enjoy them and think of happier times."

The door cracked open and Trina's hand came out. "She had a sweet tooth, my mom. Glad she got a cupcake right before... what happened."

"That was at your daughter's bridal shower, right?" I asked. "We happened to be at the Beanstalk Café when Maisie picked up the cupcakes."

Trina took the tub from Ren and permitted herself a deep sniff. "They weren't up to Renata's standards, I must admit."

"That's okay," Ren said. "The focus was on celebrating your daughter. I know Brianna... and here she is now."

It was easy to recognize Maisie's descendants as they all had her square jaw and small eyes. The harshness seemed to soften with each generation, however, and the youngest woman was quite pretty despite the sorrow etched in her face.

"I'm sorry about your grandmother's passing, Brianna," Renata said, gesturing to the treats. "I made some of her favorite things to commemorate her."

Brianna teared up. "Thank you for thinking of her. Grandma was good to me and I'll miss her."

"You'd better go," Trina said, pulling the door closed. "No use upsetting us more than we already are. There could be a killer lurking around every corner. That's what it feels like, and it was supposed to be a happy time."

"I'm sure the police will get to the bottom of it before the wedding," I said. "As kind as Maisie was to family, it seemed she had a few enemies, at least in business."

"Like you two," Trina said. "And the rest of the Brightons."

"Oh, Mom, you're just upset," Brianna said. "Grandma liked Renata. You could see it in the way she hardly dissed her. At least till lately. As for Janelle, you can't blame her for what her mom and cousin did. I wouldn't want to carry that weight in our family."

The way Brianna's shoulders slumped told me she already did. It was too much weight for a girl in her twenties just setting out in life.

I had intended to try to get a reading from Trina, but Brianna's fingers were within reach. Better yet, there was an engagement ring with perhaps the smallest diamond I'd ever seen.

"Someone's a cheapskate," Bixby offered, from my mental sidelines.

Pressing my lips together, I tried to hold back one of the natural processes he'd mentioned earlier.

"A belch of laughter is still a belch," he said, sounding delighted with himself.

I found a smile for Brianna. "Thank you for your kindness. It is hard to carry the weight of family reputation sometimes."

"Very. All I wanted was to get married and have kids, but it isn't that easy."

"It can be easy again, after the grief passes." Reaching out, I touched her hand gently, resting my index finger on the diamond chip. It wasn't just grief I felt inside Brianna, however, but also fear.

"Ouch," Bixby said. "This girl is terrified. Is Oscar after them?"

"Distract her," I muttered internally. "This could take a sec."

Mr. Bixby rose to the challenge, literally. Sitting up in my arms, he gave a heartrending whine that soared into the morning skies.

"What's wrong with him?" Brianna asked, surprise briefly replacing sadness in her eyes.

"He's expressing his condolences," I said. "Mr. Bixby is a very sensitive dog."

She smiled for the first time. "That is so sweet."

The little spark of happiness in her mind lit up in sharp contrast to the bleak landscape within. Brianna felt trapped, either by her family or— "Oh."

"What?" she asked.

"Brianna, don't get married," I blurted.

Mr. Bixby snorted. "That could have been more tactful."

"I'm sorry," I added, before she could reply. "All I mean is that you should give it some time—until you can really enjoy it. Knowing Maisie, she would have wanted the best for you."

"She... she..." Brianna stuttered to a stop.

"She didn't want you to get married either," I said. "Did she?"

Trina jerked the door, almost crushing her daughter's fingers with mine.

"Mom, stop. You know what Grandma said. She wanted me to put my career first. To use my botany degree while it's still fresh."

Flicking my fingers away, Trina pried her daughter's off the doorframe. "I know the hall and caterer are paid for. I know there's a rack of dresses sitting ready and guests with plane tickets."

"Plenty of weddings get postponed," I said. "Especially if a family is in mourning."

"Bucky would be so mad," Brianna said. "He's set on this."

"Bucky?" Bixby asked. "What kind of grown man calls himself Bucky?"

An abuser, I told him. This Bucky was manipulating both

Brianna and Trina, I sensed. Only Maisie could see through him. She wanted her granddaughter to be happy but had tried to derail the wedding.

"I'm sure Bucky would understand," I said. "Every groom wants a joyful bride."

Brianna blinked at me through the screen and I didn't need to touch her to know that joy wasn't part of her repertoire with Bucky.

Mr. Bixby cleared his throat. "I would like to be patted. By Brianna."

That was a very strange request coming from my affection-averse dachshund, so I tried to oblige. "Brianna, my dog seems to be feeling sad over what's happened. Would you give him a pat to let him know you're okay?"

Tears rolled down her cheeks as she elbowed her mother back and opened the door again. Her fingers ran over Bixby's soft black ears and down his back. For the first time, I tried to send pulses of hope and healing to someone *through* the dog.

"Ugh, enough," he said. "All that sugar is making me queasy."

He sounded rather pleased with himself nonetheless, because Brianna was standing taller and her smile was genuine. "What a wonderful dog. I'd love one just like him."

"That's a great idea," I said. "Postpone the wedding and get a dachshund. It will restore you in no time."

Trina dropped the pastries on the floor behind her and jerked her daughter back. "Get off my property, Janelle Brighton. And stop putting foolish notions in my daughter's head."

I didn't know whether Trina understood that I was indeed putting notions into Brianna's head. With any luck, this girl would send Bucky to the trash where he belonged. That would be one of the bigger accomplishments since my return.

"You have plenty of those," Bixby said, settling back onto my hip. "But I'm claiming this one as mine."

CHAPTER FIFTEEN

"I feel like I missed a lot back there," Renata said, following us down the driveway. "I wish I could hear your chitchat with Mr. Bixby."

"You don't," Bijou said. "He's a bag of brag that only gets worse in private."

"Then don't eavesdrop," Bixby said. "Braggadocio is warranted sometimes. Particularly today."

My steps slowed as I pondered our next move. "He's right. This time. What I plucked out of Brianna is that her fiancé is—"

"A turd," Bixby interjected.

"Crassy-pants," Bijou said. "Renata doesn't like your manners."

Ren laughed. "Thank you for looking out for my sensibilities, Bijou, but I'm not that delicate. Mr. Bixby has a way of getting to the point."

"Thank you for appreciating my efficiency, Renata," he said. "Flattery is always welcome, but I won't let it stop me from noticing Janelle is going rogue."

Indeed, my feet had started back up the driveway almost of their own accord. The door of the Gledhill house was closed and the curtains drawn.

"Not the greenhouse," Ren said, behind me. "It's asking for trouble."

"Not *this* greenhouse, anyway," I said.

During my previous visit, I noticed Sonia had elected to forge into the bush rather than take the driveway back to her home, despite the darkness. Obviously, she knew her way to and from the Gledhill house well—and yet she had not been friends with Maisie. Perhaps she was among the ranks of people coveting her neighbor's green thumb.

Beckoning, I slid into the sliver of a break in the shrubbery, ignoring Bixby's very audible complaints. "I prefer if Renata breaks trail," he said. "Apparently I'm the delicate one. My skin is so sensitive since my return from beyond. Or maybe I'm just more aware of it. When Brianna touched me it sent strange little shocks through my system."

"That was me, Bixby," I said. "At least, I think so. She was depleted and I was trying to fuel her up."

"Interesting," he said. "It felt prickly. Like a…" He paused and then exclaimed, "Like a big ol' sunflower passing through and out of me! Flower flatulence!"

A laugh spluttered out of me and Ren giggled, too.

Bijou broke her prim silence. "Move over, Crassy-pants. Ren and I will break trail so you can—"

"Break wind," he said, as I made way for Ren and Bijou to pass me. "That's the ideal division of labor. You'd probably be more comfortable, Bijou, if you'd just—"

"Never mind," I said. "This would be a good time for silence, Mr. Bixby. Sonia had sharp edges and we'll need to keep our wits about us."

Sonia wasn't the one to watch for, as it turned out. Long before we reached her yard, I discovered a snake.

Inside, rather than outside.

The familiar feeling of nausea made Mr. Bixby pant. "Not again. Shouldn't that man be sleeping it off in his pool house?"

"Ren, slow down," I whispered, as we caught up to her in a clearing. "Oscar Knight is in the vicinity."

She stopped abruptly and Bijou circled back to stand between us. "Stinky," she said. "Thought it was regular compost."

Bixby lifted his nose. "The poodle's right. He doesn't smell as foul as usual."

"Broken heart, I bet," I said. "It must be hard on him to be cast out of his own house."

"More like broken powers," Mr. Bixby said. "Something's gone wrong with Oscar's magic maker."

"Maybe we should turn back," I said. "Broken magic can be worse than regular magic. It's unpredictable. I know that from grim experience."

"Agreed," Ren said. "Let's try again later. Besides, Sonia might be packing a full set of powers."

Bijou lifted her slender muzzle. "Not home."

That made the decision tempting in a different way. Knowing Sonia was away meant we could take a poke around.

"Except for the fact that Oscar is already doing just that," Mr. Bixby said.

"I'm nervous about running into him," Ren said. "But whatever you think is best."

I peered through the bushes and a movement caught my eye. It wasn't about running into him anymore. It was about getting away from him. Beyond this clearing, we were surrounded by bushes that would make escape difficult.

My heart started pounding in the way it usually did when Oscar was around—so hard it was a wonder I could ever think straight.

"You don't," Mr. Bixby said, switching to our inside line. "But that's why you have me. One of many reasons."

"I can't let him corner Ren and Bijou out here," I said. "We could easily disappear."

"You could. In fact, that's exactly what I'd suggest. Disappear, and pronto."

"Bixby! I'm not leaving Ren and Bijou behind to fend for themselves, even to play invisible decoy."

He gave a strenuous wriggle, perhaps intended to ground me in the moment. "I would never suggest abandoning Ren or even the prissy poodle. What I was saying is use the spell as a cloak. Cover all of you."

Doubt flooded in instantly. "I don't think it works that way."

"It absolutely can work that way," he said. "And based on what I've experienced of your growing power, I'd say you can pull it off. Consider it an unintended gift from Liberty."

I pulled my eyes away from the movement ahead of us. Was Oscar really bushwhacking in a cashmere coat? "What if it failed and we ended up even more exposed?"

"Just focus hard on what you want to achieve. One minute you're all visible, the next gone."

"Gone. But what if we really go somewhere?"

"Like Pluto? Miss Brighton, I don't think it works that way." His chuckle was reassuring. "Get on it. You know he can tell when—"

"Hello!" Oscar's voice rang out. "I can smell you, Janelle Brighton. In case you're wondering, it reeks of moss, with a hint of stagnant water."

"Moss, exactly," Bixby said. "Isn't that what I told you? You let your powers lapse far too long."

Ignoring him, I whispered the plan to Renata. We bent in the same moment. She picked up Bijou while I set Bixby down, where he promptly vanished. Then I linked arms with Ren, imagined the clearing literally clearing, and waited for Bixby to announce, "Good job. Now, make like trees and stand there while I try to herd the silver fox away from the hens."

I thought about protesting but it was a waste of much-needed energy. Ren trembled at first, but her arms tightened around Bijou and gradually she calmed.

The thrashing in the bushes continued. "I can't smell you anymore, Janelle, but I know you're here because I still feel nauseated. We need to have a little chat, so don't go anywhere."

We waited for what felt like an eternity before he joined us in the clearing.

"I hate the wilderness," he said. "There are burrs on my coat and something keeps snagging my pants. Only sheer desperation keeps me going." He gave a surprisingly pleasant laugh. "You're a hard girl to find. I've already been to your store and even that café I should close down."

He stopped walking and stared around the clearing with his silver-gray eyes. "Come out, come out wherever you are."

It sounded like a spell, similar to the lost and found spell in my book that revealed hidden things.

"You're good," Bixby told me. "Your invisibility is holding."

Oscar cocked his head, almost as if he could hear the dog. I was confident he couldn't but decided to try reinforcing my spell anyway. I imagined an impenetrable globe encasing Renata, Bijou and me.

Reaching into his pocket, Oscar pulled out a small glass vial and tipped something into his palm. It looked like ash.

"Sunflower ash," Bixby confirmed.

This time Oscar blew some dust into the air, and repeated his spell. His grumble of frustration told me this had worked before. I wondered if his powers really had diminished or mine had grown.

"Little of both, most likely," Bixby said. "Never underestimate a vexed warlock."

With that, Oscar bent, picked up some large rocks and started hurling them in our general direction, one by one.

"Hold steady," Bixby called.

I couldn't. The very thought of Ren and Bijou being struck with sharp stones petrified me.

"Don't do it, Witchy," Bijou whispered. "Don't do it."

But I did, of course, and the hiccup broke the spell.

CHAPTER SIXTEEN

"Ah, there you are." Oscar's smile was somewhat less feral than usual, despite his clear win in the game of magic. "I was hoping you'd show yourself. Never like to hit a lady."

Luckily he was so taken with himself he didn't notice the pair of sunflowers that had sprung up a few yards behind him.

"Untrue," I said. "You hit Cousin Liberty where it counted, didn't you?"

He shrugged broad, cashmere-covered shoulders. "Liberty is no lady. The jury is still out on you. It's Renata I worried about."

I moved in front of Ren and Bijou. "I'm lady enough to shield my friends. You will leave Ren and Bijou alone, Mr. Knight."

He raised one eyebrow so finely shaped I wondered if he manscaped. "Or what, exactly? Surely you don't think you're a match for me when it comes to magic?"

"Probably not, but I have something you don't."

Walking forward relentlessly, he smiled. "Do tell. What could possibly protect you and your brat pack from me?"

I didn't hesitate to fire my secret weapon. "Octavia. I guess that's a who, not a what."

The tall man stopped suddenly. "How dare you bring up my wife at a time like this?"

"Mr. Knight. *Oscar*. I always feel awkward calling you that, but I'm going to push through it. Your wife and I have chatted. Wouldn't go so far as to say we're friends, but I expect she'd want you to leave us unharmed."

His silvery eyes narrowed to slits. "You're lying."

"If I were lying, would I know you got retired to the pool house?"

I expected him to be shocked but he just shrugged again. "So you're spying. And once you're married, you'll discover there are ups and downs."

"Sure, but this is a big down, Oscar. She gave me her rings."

He was shocked but only his Adam's apple gave it away. It bobbed twice in quick succession. "You're lying."

"Not lying. I tried to give them back to her. It makes me profoundly uncomfortable to be caught in the middle of your fight and I most certainly do not want Tavi's rings."

"Would you care to tell me why she gave them to you? Or would you like me to torture it out of you?" Turning, he stared around the clearing and found Bixby, now visible. "Starting with that stupid mutt. The living slinky."

"You won't do that, Oscar," I said. Silently, I urged Bixby to vanish and hide and for a change the dog actually obeyed. "I know you could but I doubt you would. Because you still love your wife enough to deliver tea to her every morning. Hurting an innocent dog is what got you banished in the first place."

He threw the rocks into the bushes and I held my breath, hoping a yelp wouldn't follow.

"Fine," Bixby called from much further away. "Carry on. You've got this."

"I didn't hurt Liberty's sheepdog," Oscar said. "Not intentionally. He got in the way of the spell. And then he refused to leave her. I did try, but he was ridiculously loyal. None of our dogs have ever been that loyal."

"To you," I said. "They are to Tavi."

"Don't call her that. It's too—"

"Familiar," I cut in. "I know, but that's what she wants me to call her. Oscar, you'll win her back in time, but it won't be by threatening us."

"What she doesn't know won't hurt her," he muttered, kicking at a stone with one expensive loafer.

I stared at him, realizing that was probably the code he lived by in his marriage. Octavia didn't know their son was a deadbeat. She didn't know half of the crimes her husband committed. Holding her rings told me she'd lived her life in ignorance. At first I assumed that was by her design, but now I wondered if he spent his whole life covering up misdeeds to feel worthy of his wife.

"Are you well, Oscar?" I asked. "You seem a little run down."

His eyes came up to meet mine. "The holidays are always stressful in retail. You'll see that soon enough. It wasn't great timing for Maisie to— well, you know."

"Die," I said. "Liberty likes to face that word head-on, so I will, too. And you were loitering around, so I figured you might have something to do with her untimely demise."

He shook his head. "She was an obnoxious woman, but she got a free pass with me and many others."

"Because of her skills in the greenhouse," I said.

"It always astounds me how people can be so useless in most regards and gifted in others. I can't tell you how many times people have wanted help to deal with Maisie. She charged too much. She doled out product based on whim. She'd kill a plant just to keep you from having it. But when it came to growing, she had no rival."

"I've heard there are others aspiring to fill her role in our community," I said. "Including one of your friends, actually."

"Arnold Blatchford? I've heard the rumors, and I'm sure he

wishes he could replace her. But he doesn't have the chops. He'll overpromise, underdeliver and end up as fertilizer."

"Mr. Knight!" When it came to comments like that, I couldn't use his first name. "That's a terrible thing to say."

"I'm a pragmatist, Janelle. Arnold's a friend, as far as that goes. But if he's behind what happened to Maisie, it won't work out as he hoped. That's all."

Renata poked her head out from behind me. "We've got to get going, Mr. Knight. Janelle's store opens in twenty minutes."

He didn't bother looking at her and instead caught my eye. "Then you'd better get talking."

"About what, exactly?"

"About what you were doing in the greenhouse with Liberty last night. You beat me there, and apparently you took all the product I wanted. When I got past the police there was nothing left."

"What product in particular?"

He rolled his eyes. "I want you to deliver everything you took from Maisie to my office. If you do, I'll spare your friend and dogs. No deal on Liberty."

"I expect Liberty can protect herself," I said. "She had years to do nothing but study magic so she's a match for all of your cadre."

"I very much doubt that, Janelle," he said, turning to go. "I'll see you this afternoon. There's something I need rather urgently from your ill-gotten gains."

He did a double take when he saw the twin sunflowers, now tall and strong, but kept walking.

"Oscar." He didn't turn, so I shouted, "Oscar! I didn't get it."

"Didn't get what?" he said, still walking.

"The product you want to use on your wife."

CHAPTER SEVENTEEN

"I didn't think a big man could move that fast," Bixby said, now visible at my feet. "You'd better hoist me into shield position."

Oscar faced me with eyes full of fury. "I told you once not to come between a man and his wife. Yet here you are again."

"I know what you're doing to Tavi, but I haven't told her. I never will if you back off right now and promise to leave us alone."

"Like his promise is worth anything," Mr. Bixby said.

"I don't make promises," he said. "They're too much trouble to keep."

I smiled. "There's something vaguely honorable about that, but I'm going to need one from you now. And know that if you kill me, I've made sure Octavia will find out exactly what you're doing."

His pupils seemed to contract to mere slits, leaving way too much silver for my comfort. "You're bluffing."

"I don't bluff, because I don't always have the goods to back it up. Yet. But if your goal is to make things up with your wife, I'm going to suggest you find the plants you need elsewhere. Liberty apparently knows people who know people. Maybe you can have a chat and get yourself hooked up."

Pulling a handkerchief from his pocket, he shook it hard and then mopped his brow. It was a very cool day but perspiration ran down his cheeks. "As if she'd tell me anything."

"Oh, you know how these things go. You give her something and she'll give you something. For the moment, I'd say you need a little something for your own medicine kit. You look awful. No offense."

He glared at me over the handkerchief. "Offense taken. I'm fine."

I turned to Bijou, whose nose indicated otherwise. "Not so fine, snake man."

"Have you thought about poison?" I asked. "You were behind the extermination spell used against us. Maybe someone's turned the tables."

"Hold up, Janelle," Mr. Bixby said. "If someone's exterminating Oscar, isn't that a good thing? I mean, life would be easier if he weren't ambushing us all the time."

"I'm not being poisoned." Oscar shifted uneasily as he pondered. "I'd know."

Mr. Bixby leaned over and took a long sniff. "The poodle's right. Decomp."

"I have reason to think otherwise, Oscar. There's a foul odor— one that goes beyond the usual. You're currently rotting from the inside out."

The handkerchief patted faster. "That's impossible. No one has that kind of access to me."

"Are you sure?" I asked. "It takes less than you'd think."

He came so close that even I could pick up the distinctive odor of decomposition. "Are you suggesting my wife is poisoning me? Because if you are, I'd have to kill you right now."

I knew he meant it. His pent-up desire to deal with the Brighton problem was palpable. But that's not why I had to take this head-on. Letting him think Tavi was poisoning him would put her in peril.

"It's not your wife, sir." Lifting one hand, I gestured for him to step back. "For whatever reason, she still loves you, so I suggest you focus on getting yourself healthy and proving you're worthy of her."

"I don't take advice from novice witches who don't know anything."

"I know enough to cure you, Oscar, because I cured myself. It's not pleasant, I admit. How's the plumbing in the pool house?"

"I don't need your help." He turned in disgust and started to walk away again, this time taking a moment to kick the sunflowers hard enough to make him hop. The flowers barely swayed, bouncing upright immediately.

"Okay, but if you change your mind, we can clear those pipes for you. With Maisie gone, we might need to get creative."

Stopping at the edge of the clearing, he mopped his face and shook his head in bewilderment. "Why couldn't you have just—"

"Died the first time you tried? Or the second? Or even the third?" I shrugged. "I can only conclude there's a grand plan for us, Oscar. Maybe it starts with me saving your life."

"I'd rather die." He balled up the handkerchief and threw it at me.

"What a sad sight," Mr. Bixby said. "A warlock reduced to throwing hankies instead of curses."

"Pride," I told the dog. "I had to ditch plenty of it before coming home." I waited till the man was nearly out of earshot before trying again. "Call me if you change your mind, Oscar. I'd do it for free, for Tavi. But if your pride needs to make a deal out of it, there are a few things I could ask for in return."

He turned and stared long and hard, and I thought he was going to crack. "At one point, I said you were difficult to dislike, Janelle. Turns out I was wrong."

CHAPTER EIGHTEEN

I turned the sign on Whimsy's door to "open" at 11 o'clock sharp.

"At least something's sharp, because you've looked better," Mr. Bixby said. "Obviously, you've looked far worse, too."

"Thanks so much, pal," I said, taking him off the counter and setting him on the floor. I wouldn't dream of disciplining this dachshund like a regular dog but that didn't mean I needed to tolerate insults at waist level. He could fire them up from below.

"You're being silly. I can fire them off inside your head," he pointed out, clicking over to the best of the sunbeams. With the late November chill setting in, he took advantage of all available heat sources—even Bijou—when the going got tough. He wasn't big on the idea of coats and sweaters, however, and was full of stories about bigger dogs mistaking sweatered dogs for stuffed toys.

"Not stories," he said now, flinging himself down so hard his tags jangled. "Truth. A dog the size of Atticus could deploy the same move I used on rodents. How would you feel then?"

"Well, right now the only thing he moves is books. It's a little strange when you come to think of it. Harold was blustering around like a crazy typhoon when he was a ghost."

"Hairball was and is a witch's dog. Atticus is just an average mutt."

"Far from average. You four are special, no doubt about that."

I walked over to the shelves and started straightening the very products I had already arranged just so. It was one of my greatest joys to move things around, always looking for the best configuration to showcase them. Something was working, because nothing stuck around for long. My suppliers were still scarce but it meant more eyeballs on Sinda's jewels, which were the main event anyway. She was working downstairs now on her very popular puppy pendants. They were not part of the ghost dog line, but people loved them and had started to place orders for specific breeds. Dachshunds were among the most popular.

"I prefer to be in a class by myself," Bixby said. "Special."

I tossed my shammy at him and he didn't flinch, let alone move. It missed anyway.

"You know what I'm going to do before I do it. That's about as special as it gets." Stooping to pick up the shammy, I asked, "Were you a witch's dog, too? If you don't mind my asking."

"I do mind. There's a code, you know. It requires the strictest of confidentiality."

"Ah. Okay. Well, I suppose that will work in my favor when you move on to help the next hapless magical individual. You'll keep my secrets."

He chuckled. "You don't even keep your secrets. If you're hiccupping sunflowers for Drew, it's all out there."

"I have a few secrets. Not many. It would be too hard to remember them."

He lifted his head. "That's where a brilliant familiar like me comes in handy. I have an encyclopedic mind. I prefer to know everything and file it accordingly."

"And use it to browbeat me." I stooped to pat his speckled belly before heading back to the counter. "It's one of the things I love about you. Keeps me humble."

Flipping back, he cocked his head. "It's a fine balance between keeping you humble enough to be alert and cocky enough to take chances. Not just any dog could pull off my job. Bijou would be obsequious and Harold dismissive. Then where would you be?"

"Confused. At least, more confused. I do depend on your sage advice, Mr. Bixby. Today I wouldn't have thought to try cloaking Ren and Bijou with invisibility and it's something that could save their lives down the road."

"When you get those hiccups reined in." He collapsed on his side again. "I don't blame you for that. It's Liberty's fault. No good deed goes unpunished."

"I'll get it under control. In the meantime, we've got a different sort of problem with Oscar."

"He'll still try to kill you, make no mistake," the dog said. "He'll just be sneakier about it knowing Tavi has your back. After all, he's successfully kept her from knowing the depravity of her own son."

"I wonder if he's dosing her with something on top of the rangleroot."

"To keep her stupid?" Bixby asked.

"She's just naïve. At least I think so." I sighed. "Oscar's intentions are probably good as far as Tavi is concerned. His enemies would use her vulnerability against him."

"Just as he used Harold against Liberty."

"I don't know about that. He almost had me convinced otherwise today. But in his current state, nothing he says can be taken at face value."

Bixby got to his feet and paced. He liked hearing the click of his claws on hardwood as much as I did heels. "So he's doping his wife with the morning tea she sees as a romantic gesture."

"I suppose it is a romantic gesture. He's keeping her safe."

"Piffle. The best way to keep her safe would be to behave

himself. Instead he sails through town riling people up and creating risk for her."

I directed an index finger at him. "Good point. Very good point."

"Which you'd have made yourself if you weren't so tired. But I'm happy to pick up the slack when you're slacking."

"So he's dosing her with at least a protective spell and possibly also a memory spell. Do we even know the real Tavi?"

"Does he?" Bixby asked. "She may have already been spelled by her own mother when he met her. Maybe she isn't as nice as she seems."

I thought about that. "You can fake a lot of things but not loving a dog. At least, not to me. Not to us."

He lifted his paw in my direction, mimicking me. "Good point. Very good point."

"What a team," I said, and we both laughed.

If we hadn't been so busy congratulating ourselves, we might have noticed someone watching outside the window.

Instead, we both jumped when the doorbell gave a strangled screech.

CHAPTER NINETEEN

S onia Dinogue looked better in daylight—or at least the soft light that filtered into Whimsy. I wondered if someone had charmed the windows of my store because everything looked better in here. My friends shone like the jewels on display and the dogs' coats had a rich luster. Liberty seemingly got younger with her visits. Of course, some of that was attributable to the energy she borrowed from me.

"Stole," Bixby said, inside my head. "Borrowed suggests an intention to return it. You can bet that won't happen."

"Welcome to Whimsy," I said. "I'm Janelle Brighton, the owner."

"I know who you are," Sonia said, pulling her hat down with both hands. It was a worn blue felt cloche with a limp flower on the side. "And I know you were on my property earlier. I have cameras trained on every square inch."

So this wasn't a retail opportunity. I could drop one mask and put on another.

"And pick up your dog shield, if I may suggest," Mr. Bixby said. "Something tells me you're going to need it."

I did as he suggested and then met Sonia's eyes. They were

hazel and the fringe of hair under the hat was still quite dark. "You're right, Miss Dinogue. I came over to visit you after speaking to Trina and Brianna Peck."

She spun her hand as a signal to continue. "Go on. I don't have all day."

"You weren't home, it seems."

"How would you know? You never made it to the door. Instead, you and Renata were kibitzing in the woods with Oscar Knight. A most unlikely trio, I must say."

"Not *that* unlikely," I said. "Mr. Knight is on the Christmas committee with me, and his wife is one of my best customers. It happened that he was leaving your place and told me you weren't home."

"And then you discussed Christmas decorations, I suppose." Her expression was mocking. "You and Oscar were in the bush talking twinkle lights."

"We do have differing views on that subject. I believe there can never be enough twinkle lights and Oscar balks at the cost to the town."

"I see. Oscar certainly got worked up over it. He was whipping that hankie around like a damsel in distress."

I fought a grin. "He has a bit of a cold, it seems. And he was upset to have missed you."

"What would he want with me?" she asked. "For that matter, what did *you* want with me?"

"I can only speak for myself, Miss Dinogue." Walking over to the window, I closed the blinds. Technically it was too late. Martha Wentwhistle, of the Main Street Posse, had walked by slowly, peering into the store. "I heard you had a greenhouse and wanted to talk to you about it. I'm in the market for some botanicals."

"My greenhouse is small and my plants aren't for sale. Not to you, not to Oscar. They're for personal use, only."

"Then perhaps you'd consider donating a seedling to me. I'm looking to grow some rangleroot at the Brighton manor."

She reared back. "Rangleroot is not for amateurs, young lady. It's more sensitive than Goldilocks. The greenhouse can't be too warm or too cold. The lighting and humidity have to be just right. One chill breeze and you're wiped out." She mumbled under her breath. "If someone hasn't wiped you out first."

"Did someone steal your rangleroot?" I asked. "Because I understand it's in short supply."

Pacing around the shop on dirty sneakers, she stared at the jewelry with glazed eyes. "It's always in short supply, and now even shorter. I wish people would think before they snatch because it's not easily replaced. Especially for small operators."

"Is it always in high demand?" I asked.

"Steady. It's a mainstay, I suppose." She turned back to me and her eyes cleared. "I assumed Oscar had helped himself to my supply, but perhaps not since he was there today. My next best guess is your cousin, Liberty."

"She's just back from visiting my gran down south. I don't believe she's had time to check her medicine cabinet."

I wondered how much Sonia would share about what she knew and it looked like she was struggling internally. "Janelle," she said at last, "I know Liberty was found standing over Maisie's dead body. And that you were with her." She did another turn around the store. "I always figured someone would get to Maisie, but you and Liberty weren't on my list of suspects. I thought she was dead and that someone would kill you before you ever got back."

"Nice," Bixby said. "Can I fade out and give her a little nip?"

I told him to stand down and found a smile for Sonia. "I appreciate your candor. Liberty and I are innocent and that will be proven before long. I wasn't aware Maisie had so many enemies."

Sonia sniffed. "She was the worst kind of neighbor. Never thought twice about roaming around my property and pillaging my wildflowers. Yet she set up traps to keep me from doing the same on hers."

"Traps? What kind of traps?"

"Oh, it varied depending on mood. Bear traps, concealed caverns, rope snares, and especially botanical. I could barely keep up with the rashes. Just a molecule of the wrong weed and your skin goes up in flames." She scratched her arms absently. "I had to keep a whole line of plants to counteract her shenanigans."

I wondered how we'd managed to miss these traps and a canine grumble suggested Bixby and Bijou had helped us avoid at least some of them.

"It was still worth it to forage?" I asked. "For both of you?"

"There were other ways to find what we needed but we both had a green thumb and specialized in different things. It was handy to forage, as you say, although it came at a price." Catching my eye, she smirked. "Maisie lost all her fingernails on swamp thistle she tried to steal from my land. Took a year to grow back."

"Gives a whole new meaning to turf wars," I said. "I suppose you're relieved she's gone."

"Relieved? Hardly. I didn't like Maisie but I admired her. A worthy adversary." She walked to the door. "Besides, the devil you know is always better than the devil you don't." The bell overhead rattled almost nervously and she stared up at it. "Why do you want rangleroot, Janelle? It's not for novices like you."

"Apparently it has protective powers. That sounds pretty appealing to this novice."

She pulled the door open a crack. "Understandable. But it's too precious to be squandered like that."

"I suppose, but I'd still like to try. Can I find it on the internet?"

"Sure, you can." A breeze blew through the crack in the door. It lifted the hair on my arms and ruffled Bixby's fur. "Definitely a case of buyer beware. Do you have any idea of how many witches die each year from sheer ignorance?"

"Uh, no." It was a little shocking to hear the "w" word drop so easily from her lips.

"Because she sees you as an equal," Mr. Bixby said, silently.

"She said I was a novice," I replied.

"A novice who's equal in power, and therefore to be watched. But Sonia's probably right about buying online. Based on my experience, one plant can so easily pass for another."

"Too many," Sonia said, about the number of ignorant witches. "More than anyone ever admits."

"Hence the high demand for rangleroot for protection," I said. "What a shame it's in such short supply."

Her teeth showed in a benign smile as she stepped outside. "I bow to the person who can farm it properly. It's pure gold in our world."

"Are you going to visit Oscar, too?" I asked, sticking my head out the door.

Sonia made a slashing motion across her lips. "Don't call that name on Main Street, silly witch. You have no idea what little it takes to get..."

"Killed?" I suggested, when her voice trailed off.

"I was going to say a bad reputation. But then I realized you had that from the jump. It comes with the Brighton name."

"Thanks for stopping by," I said, sending my best smile after her. "Do come back for your Christmas shopping."

Pushing into the wind, she called back, "Coal for everyone this year. Again."

CHAPTER TWENTY

At two, I turned the sign to closed for lunch, buttoned Bixby and myself into coats, and set off on some errands.

"By errands, I hope you mean further investigation," the dog said. "This had better be worth a coat because I'm roasting like a Thanksgiving turkey."

"Which reminds me to talk to Ren about Thanksgiving," I said. "It's in a few days and we have no plans."

"We have plans to get your cousin off the hook for murder. Isn't that enough for a family holiday?"

I hurried down the sidewalk, clicking nicely in my best stiletto boots. Renata had kindly run home to collect a change of clothes for me and I felt more like myself again. From now on, I'd be sure to keep some options in the back room to be ready for anything.

"When you put it that way, I guess so," I told the dog. "But I owe it to Sinda and Ren to do better. They haven't celebrated in years, whereas I was always living it up at one resort or another."

"Artificial joy," he said. "You want this holiday for yourself as much as your friends."

"I guess. It's the first time I've felt I've had a home in more than a decade. A home and the best friends in the world. That's something worth celebrating."

"Even if someone is constantly trying to kill you?"

"Especially if someone is constantly trying to kill me. I need to enjoy the small things."

"Cooking a turkey is not a small thing. Based on my observations. They generally outweigh me by several magnitudes."

I adjusted his position and scratched his head. "Can we not talk about you in the same breath as turkey? My stomach is nearly always queasy here. Never fully recovered from poisoning."

"Is that why you went so easy on Oscar earlier?"

"Easy? I thought I was hard on him." We stopped in front of the Beanstalk Café. It wasn't my primary destination but I couldn't help looking for Atticus. The beautiful white dog was not only there but sitting among a scattering of books. "It's about Octavia. I suppose I'm a romantic. As reprehensible as we find Oscar, she loves him."

"Doesn't count if she's too stoned on his spells to know him," he said. "Maybe he drugged her into marrying him."

"Free will," I said. "In fact, her engagement ring told me she went against her parents' wishes and eloped with him."

"Ooooh, forbidden love," the dog said. "I'm a sucker for stories like that."

"Not me," I said. "I like my happily ever afters."

He snickered under my arm. "You know you're in the wrong line of work for that. How many happy 'w' words do you know?"

I opened the door to the café and switched seamlessly to internal dialogue. "How about Sinda and Renata?"

"They're just starting out in the world of magical peril. But your mom? Liberty? And their ancestors? No rainbows and unicorns for them."

My steps slowed as I walked to the counter and joined a short line. He wasn't wrong.

"I never am," he said. "I saw too much during my last tour of duty."

"Which you don't want to discuss."

"Correct. But I'll consider it if you get me a biscotti. I like the crunch."

Valerie lit up when she saw me as if it were a rare sighting, when I'd actually become a frequent flyer. "Business is picking up, Janelle. I'm so excited."

"It was the free muffins," I said. "Even in Wyldwood, no one passes that up."

"I'm starting to wonder if the little issue I consulted you about is actually more good luck than bad."

"Awesome!" I moved down the counter to wait for a fresh pot of coffee to finish brewing. When I got to the bookshelf, I stooped to replace the books Atticus had knocked out. *Romeo and Juliet* and *Anna Karenina*.

Tragic love stories.

"That's got to be a coincidence, right?" I asked Bixby.

"Probably. This dog looks too dopey to yank super-sobbers deliberately. He's more of a slapstick guy. No subtlety whatsoever."

Neither of the books had seen much wear and tear. Their covers were pristine because few had elected to read them while enjoying a beverage over the years. I smoothed a couple of dogeared pages and put them back in alphabetical order.

"Atticus, I know you're bored but could you find another hobby?" I asked. "Books are treasures to me."

"You were a terrible student," Bixby said. "At least according to my tours of your private records. Those report cards made you sound vacuous."

"I just preferred keeping a low profile. Reading was always my escape of choice. Low risk. Mostly."

"You singed a couple," he said, "according to my sniff around your bookcase."

I gave him a look. "Accidents. I'm making up for it here."

He turned away and then snickered. "Don't look now. Old Mr. Trench Coat is keeping his eye on you and his crossword puzzle at the same time. You scared him by threatening to hurl hot dogs."

"Hot dogs?" I continued to straighten the books as we waited. "You're okay with that term?"

"Uh, no. I've reconsidered. Into the lexicon with the rest of the tubular meats."

I couldn't help laughing out loud and then my eyes inevitably jumped to the old man at his regular table.

"Out of the frying pan and into the fire," Bixby said. "That's how hiccups happen."

"Then stop making me laugh," I said, internally, managing a smile for Valerie as she slid a coffee cup across the counter.

"Impossible. I'm just that witty."

I picked up a lid and tried to put it on the steaming cup with one hand.

Mr. Bixby grumbled a protest. "Four on the floor, thank you very much. This jacket is made of some synthetic that could melt and burn my sensitive skin."

Bending, I set him down and used both hands to seal the lid. Atticus seized that opportunity to flick *Wuthering Heights* off the top shelf, and it crashed to the floor. Bixby leapt nimbly aside, yapping canine curses of the old-school variety.

"How dare he?" Mr. Bixby sputtered. "I could have been crushed! I'm prepared to sacrifice myself for your cause, but not in a drive-by book bash."

I knelt to pat my disgruntled dachshund, speaking aloud but quietly to Atticus. "Not funny, Atticus, nor the act of a gentleman. If you want my help, you'd better treat my best friend with care."

The setter had the decency to look abashed as I put the book back where it belonged. I reached out to give him a pat, but stopped with my hand hanging.

"Don't look," Bixby said. "Why touch a hot stove when you know it burns?"

I looked. The old man in the trench coat was filling in his crossword with swift, confident strokes of the pen. There was a smile—perhaps even a smirk—on his face that got wider as I drew back my hand and rose to my feet.

"Never mind," I said. Out loud and deliberately this time. "Forty-two down: private."

This time he made no secret about staring and his smirk faded.

Chin up, I strutted out of the café.

"The heels really do make a difference," Bixby said. "Someone should invent a line for height-challenged dogs."

I breathed a sigh of relief as we headed up the street. "Maybe that could be you."

"In my next life, perhaps," he said. "Because this one is about to get very tense again."

CHAPTER TWENTY-ONE

E ternal Springs Realty was conveniently located between the Beanstalk Café and Whimsy. I could see my old school chum, Mindy Tang, sitting at her desk so I walked right in. She winced slightly as she looked up but that quickly changed to a professional smile. It wasn't her fault she was stuck in the middle between Oscar Knight, who owned much of the property on Main Street, and me, the upstart who practically tricked him out of the trio of stores we bought.

"Hey, Mindy," I said, pretending she was happy to see me. It was funny how few people were, really, and such a contrast to my old life, where I was often the most popular staffer at any resort.

"It's easy to be popular when you're playing a role," Mr. Bixby said. "Harder to be authentic and accept the consequences."

I gave him a little squeeze to request that he shut off his commentary. It was rarely effective but worth a try before doing the harder work of pinching the internal communication line closed. The pressure that bubbled up behind the pinch point felt like—

"Flower flatulence," he suggested. "My witticisms are like your hiccups: uncontrollable."

"Untrue," I shot back. "You can control them but you prefer to indulge yourself."

"Maybe the same is true of your sunflowers. Ever think about that? Maybe it just feels good to erupt in yellow petals at inappropriate times."

I took a deep, calming breath and pinched off the conversation. It was tougher than many tasks in my new magical life, and good practice.

"Are you okay, Janelle?" Mindy asked. "You look a little tired."

"Sleepless night," I said. "I'm sure you heard what happened."

She nodded and her sleek black bob caught the light. Normally I was happy enough with my riot of curls but Mindy had always given me a bad case of hair envy. Knowing your hair could look the same every single day regardless of weather would save time and worry. These days, I valued predictability more than ever because I'd never had less of it.

"There's been a lot of foot traffic," she said. "It's dying down." She blinked a couple of times. "That didn't come out right."

"It's okay. No one knows what to say when these things happen. Especially me, since I seem to get caught in the crossfire. Mr. Knight likes it that way."

Mindy glanced quickly at the photo on her desk of her two children. Perhaps she was reminding herself that Oscar was her biggest client. When I spoke to her previously, she said working for him was building her kids' college fund. I had felt her terror, but she endured it to be a good mom. Life was full of tough choices.

"I suppose you're here to see if we've had any interest in your empty retail space," she said. "And I'm sorry to say the answer is still no. We do get calls but it never amounts to much."

The tenant in my neighboring store had been a florist there for well over a decade, but Oscar had made her an offer she couldn't refuse in a neighboring town. Then he scared off any potential businesses with a goal of making me sell the building back to him.

Liberty had taken the edge off my fear by promising she wouldn't let that happen. She'd emerged from her terrible magical sickness with a secret stash Oscar didn't know about.

"That's a shame," I said. "It's a beautiful space for the right person. I'd love to get another florist in there and be sandwiched by Ren's baking and beautiful blooms."

"The right person will come. They always do. Just like..."

Her voice trailed off and I finished for her. "Just like me and the former Mabel's Fables. I hope it doesn't take that long."

"It won't. There were so many rumors about your store that you've proven unfounded."

Mr. Bixby shook with laughter that was only silent because I'd pinched off his communication outlet.

"That's right. It's quite peaceful there. My refuge in this crazy world."

She sank into her seat and I leaned across her desk to pick up the family photo. "Hard to believe your girls are so big when we're the same age."

"Twins help," she said. "Got it done in one fell swoop. I recommend it, although it was a tough few years."

"I'll bet." I ran my finger along the frame. "You're having another?"

"What? No!" Her face flushed. "We can't afford it. Raising kids is expensive."

I angled the photo and shrugged. "I can't help imagining a third, Mindy. You know I was always a good guesser. That got me through school."

What actually got me through school was an excellent memory, and a talent for sensing what would be on the test. Otherwise, I'd have never made the cut for college. I was highly unmotivated when it came to academics.

"I think you're wrong this time," she said. "Things are just becoming manageable at home, which is great because work is busy.

We're in a hot market right now." Glancing away, she added, "Aside from your store. Again, I'm sorry."

"Don't be. The right person will come along and it needs to be a perfect fit for Ren and me." I put the photo back, deliberately grazing her diamond ring, which had been generous with impressions before. "I'm sure you already have your hands full. I bet you're fighting off suitors for Maisie's property."

Mindy was so startled she jumped and knocked my hand aside. But not before I saw a queue longer than the one in the Beanstalk earlier. Oscar Knight was no surprise. Sonia Dinogue, a little more so. The portly man in a suit would probably turn out to be Arnold Blatchford. I caught a glimpse of another man I didn't recognize and a woman I most certainly did: Cousin Liberty.

"It makes me so uncomfortable when people come calling in these situations," Mindy said.

"Of course. Maisie's funeral is on hold and her family may not even want to sell."

I didn't need to touch her to know that they did. Or at least, Trina Peck did. I couldn't tell if she needed the money or just wanted to offload painful memories.

Mindy got to her feet and came around the desk. "I have an appointment in a few minutes. But I promise to call you the very moment someone shows interest in the store."

"It might only be a few days, now," I said. "Don't quote me on that, but my 'guesser' is jangling like a slot machine."

Mindy laughed for the first time as she herded me out. "I wish I had a guesser like that."

I turned as I opened the door. "That's what you have me for. So I'm going to guess baby boy."

Her cheeks reddened again. "Janelle, stop. That's not on my radar."

"Not till next year," I said. "Do me a favor and don't name him Oscar."

"Goodness, no." There was a note of horror in her voice. "Honestly, Janny, you've always had a way of getting me flustered."

"That's because my guesser picked your husband for you, when he was just the new kid in school."

She leaned on the doorframe and sighed. "I always wondered if I steered things that way unconsciously."

"Any complaints so far?" I asked, grinning.

"None. But it's a hard pass on the baby boy."

I laughed as I walked off. "Over that, you have some control, old friend."

CHAPTER TWENTY-TWO

After Whimsy closed, Ren and Sinda joined me to drive over to Liberty's home in Kempville.

"Can you believe she's sharking around Maisie's property while still a suspect in the murder?" I said. "Doesn't she care how it looks?"

Mr. Bixby was conspicuously silent before finally saying, "Oh, am I allowed to talk now?"

I rolled my eyes. "You've been lamenting your brief conversational recess for hours. I wouldn't have to do it if you'd just agree to simmer down when I need to focus."

"I simmer down when *I* need to focus. Isn't that good enough? When I focus, you focus and we're all good."

I added a sigh to the eye roll. "There will come a time when I can focus on several things at once, including your witticisms. That happy day hasn't arrived."

"It'll arrive faster with practice. Just like suppressing the hiccups."

Elsa glided like a queen along the quiet roads. It was nice that one of my familiars was compliant.

"This car is not a familiar," he said. "It's a sack of bolts sprinkled with rust."

"The capacity to hold your commentary will arrive faster with practice. Just like suppressing hiccups."

"I hate it when you argue." The voice came from the back seat and was decidedly plaintive. "It stresses Renny-ren-ren."

"I'm okay, Bijou," Renata said. "But I'd be happier if you were up front with me."

The poodle flopped onto her side beside Sinda. "No room for me with all that hot air."

"Sorry for my share of it, Bijou," I said. "I'll simmer down now. Won't pay to come at Liberty too hard. She tends to smite first and ask questions later."

Ren laughed. "Liberty would never smite you."

"She might, even accidentally. If I can't control her nervous hiccups, you can be sure she can't drive my firepower. I bet she's shocking things right, left and center."

"And I bet she's practicing," Bixby said. "Liberty knows the value of hard work. Mastery."

I pulled up in front of the house. It was a replica of my family manor, complete with turret. Another cousin had built it and Liberty had bought back the property when she emerged from Oscar's killing spell.

"She's not here mastering my powers right now," I said. "The place is dark."

"But not empty," Bijou said, standing and lifting her muzzle to the window I always cracked for her.

I turned to look at the poodle. "Is Liberty home?"

"Nope. She smells like cayenne pepper mixed with cloves. Not as bad as it sounds. Piquant. Distinctive."

"And what is it you're smelling now?" I asked.

"Poisoned roadkill. With a hint of decomp."

Putting the car in reverse, I quickly backed into the shadows. "You're saying Oscar Knight is here?"

"Mr. Stinkbomb himself," she said. "Going downhill. He should have said yes to your help."

"We should call the police," Ren said. "Tell them he's broken into Liberty's home. He must be lying in wait."

Bijou pushed through the seats and planted herself on top of Mr. Bixby. His hot air diminished in the presence of her greater knowledge. When it came to toxic smells, she had him beat and he conceded the field.

"Get off me," he said, squirming out from under her fluff. "Anyone can tell Oscar's on the move. Even Janelle, if she'd take a reading."

I did just that and felt the imaginary snakes writhe. Normally I didn't need to go looking for inner signs of Oscar. Nausea should have signaled me back at the last turn.

"He is low on power," I said. "I can barely sense him."

"Liberty probably has the house secured," Bixby said. "That's why she had a handbag full of plants at Maisie's. She took what he wanted and he probably came to collect."

"Should we confront him?" I asked. "If he's weak, it might be our chance."

Bijou mumbled a negative. "Still smells like trouble."

"Besides, we already confronted him once today and got his hankie in a twist," Ren said. "Why push our luck?"

"It would be good to have backup," Sinda said. "At times like this, I do miss Shelley."

I didn't disagree out loud but I was glad Mom wasn't here. She'd get in Oscar's face and we'd all end up imprisoned here, as Liberty had been. It was a fate I didn't want for myself, let alone my friends.

There was a movement at the side of Liberty's house, where the previous owners' trampoline used to be. The gate opened and a tall man stepped through.

I leaned across Ren and the dogs and snapped a few photos. There wasn't much light but Oscar was unmistakable. He was shrouded in a faint glow.

"Rot," Bijou said. "He's leaking."

Since I was still leaning on them, we all shuddered together.

"Would you mind?" Bixby said. "I'm the one in peril of suffocation under your pile-on."

I straightened and we all watched as Oscar walked along the curb in the opposite direction. The white line made it obvious that he was weaving like a drunk.

"I feel like I should warn Octavia," I said. "He's sick but he's probably too proud to tell her."

"Or maybe she's the one poisoning him," Bixby said. "And she might do the same to you."

"She wouldn't poison Oscar," I said.

Ren turned to look at me. "She might if she gave up on getting the rangleroot. If it meant saving her dog."

"And emptying the pool house of unwanted pests," Sinda added.

I thought about it and shook my head. "Even if Tavi wanted to poison her husband, I doubt she could. She doesn't have enough magic in her to make it work."

"You said you sensed a spark," Mr. Bixby said. "I felt it, too."

"Definitely something, but not enough for that. He's a powerful man and it would take a powerful poison. If she had access to a spell and the ingredients, I still doubt she could pull it off."

Bixby thought about it and finally agreed. "She might not have the capacity herself but she has the means to get it done, no?"

"You mean hire a hit man?" I asked. "Sure. I guess."

"I was thinking more like a hit woman," Bixby said. "A savvy one, with green eyes just like yours." He gave Bijou another shove. "What do you smell, poodle?"

"Cayenne," she answered. "With cloves."

"Piquant," I said, opening the car door. "And about as pleasant as it sounds."

———

WE WERE STANDING on the front porch when a cab pulled up. Harold got out and blew up a good wind before Liberty followed.

"Well, good evening," she said. "What a lovely surprise. I hope you brought dinner because there isn't a thing in the house."

"You don't eat?" I asked, as she brushed past me with the Aussie.

"As little as possible. It slows me down." She muttered a spell at the door before using a key. We started to follow and she held up her hand. "Wait. There's another spell or two that aren't good for you."

"They weren't good for Oscar either," I said. "He looked a little haggard when he left."

She turned quickly, her face eerie in the light cast by my phone. "Oscar was here?"

"Might still be around," I said. "Can you finish dismantling your security system and let us inside?"

Only when the hall light went on did I dare to pass with Ren, Sinda and the dogs. We hadn't been here since the night we set Liberty free and I felt a trace of trauma tighten my chest.

"More than a trace," Bixby said, using our inside line. "You're leaking like Oscar. Only you smell better, in case that offends your vanity."

He managed to make me smile, which went a long way to reduce the trauma. "See?" he said. "That's why it's good not to shut me down."

"I can hear you two chattering," Liberty said, leading us into the kitchen. "Not the words, but the gist of it. The dog is being disrespectful."

"To me, not you," I said. "You really don't have any food?"

"No, and I refuse to bring in takeout."

"Because it might be poisoned," Bixby said.

She gave a slight nod. "In the old days, I could tell, of course. I'm still getting used to the new flora."

"There's new flora?" Ren asked.

"Genetically modified, like everything else these days. It's impossible to know exactly how something will work until you test it thoroughly." Leaning against the counter, Liberty crossed her arms. "Thank goodness no one can do much to change a mineral."

"They're making diamonds in a lab now," Sinda said. "Most people can't tell the difference."

"Luckily we can. They're a witch's best friend." Liberty gestured to the living room. "I kept up with the world as much as possible via TV. Sometimes Harold and I managed to do a little surfing online but an Aussie's strengths don't lie in keyboard wizardry."

"You were doing your homework," I said. "Bixby said you would."

Her green eyes twinkled. "I may have been homeschooled but my mother was a drill sergeant and I'm highly self-motivated."

Harold stared up at her raptly, which told me more than her words. The Aussie turned to pin me with a sharp gaze and the next thing I knew his hoarse voice was in my head. "She's a diamond in the rough. You got all the polish."

My lips twitched as I looked up and found Mr. Bixby and Liberty eyeing me suspiciously. "Who were you talking to?" she asked. "I felt it."

"I've got a few questions for you, first," I countered.

Ren moved past us and opened the fridge. "Eggs. Cheese. Broccoli. How about an omelet, ladies?"

Liberty shook her head. "If Oscar got in here it could be tainted."

Bijou stepped forward and delicately sniffed each item in turn before announcing, "You're good. Better than—"

I sent the poodle a silent message to hold that thought. Whether or not Liberty was behind Oscar's illness, she likely wouldn't hesitate to finish him off in a hurry. As much as I wanted him out of my life—out of Wyldwood permanently—I didn't want him murdered. Nor did I want anyone in my family on the hook for it.

"An omelet would be nice, Ren," I said. "Meanwhile, Liberty and I can have a little sit down."

I gestured to the kitchen table and she demurred. "I don't sit often anymore. I spent thirty years on my behind so I like to keep moving."

Pushing herself off the counter, she walked into the living room and I followed. The wing chairs that had flanked the fireplace and been the site of a magical confrontation were gone now, whether with the Skinner family or into a dumpster. In fact, the room was largely unfurnished, except for an oak steamer trunk and a desk with a full computer setup. A huge TV covered most of a wall and one lonely wooden chair sat in front of it.

"Central command," Mr. Bixby said, struggling to get down. When he was on his feet, he caught my eye. "Just so you know, private conversations with Harold break our code of ethics."

"Tell him, not me," I replied.

The dachshund looked up at the larger dog and decided against it. Harold was mellow tonight but there was always a cyclone in the wings. He could whisk my dog into the air and snap him like a potato chip.

"I don't appreciate the analogy," Mr. Bixby said. "I'll be over there if you need me."

Liberty walked to the computer and ran her fingers over it. "I don't know how you manage to juggle so many conversations. It's like a constant clamor in my head and I can't stand it. That's why I left the Brighton manor and came home. No offense to you and your friends."

"None taken," I said. "It was like that for me right through my twenties. Now I can mostly pick and choose what I want to hear."

"Exactly," Bixby said, still on our inside line. "You chose to take Harold's call."

"I'll always take your calls first," I told him. "But I welcome input from all the dogs I rescued. It only makes sense and you know it, Bixby."

Liberty touched her forehead, probably lost in the din. "I hope I'll learn to filter quickly because I'm not a young woman. And I can't afford distractions."

"Not when you're a suspect in a murder investigation," I said, watching as she crossed to the trunk and ran her fingers over that, too. She wasn't touching it, just hovering. "Maybe distraction is what made you implicate yourself further today. Mindy Tang told me you went into their office to inquire about Maisie's property."

Liberty shrugged. "Along with half the town, I'd imagine. Properties like that don't come along often."

"Cousin Liberty, coveting that property gives you a motive for murder."

"Again, along with half the town."

"But you were the one caught in her greenhouse holding her plants."

"Plants the police never saw," she said, passing in front of me and going into the dining room.

"Hey!" I said, following. "That's our dining room set."

"Didn't you miss it?" she asked. "It's been gone for weeks. I hired someone to move it before I went down south."

"Give it back," I said. "We need it for Thanksgiving dinner. Besides, Mom will notice the dining room at home is empty."

"Shelley owes me for running down there and dealing with Bridie's problem. I didn't even brag about it. Yet." She continued running her fingers over the furniture and then smiled. "Maybe I got some of your people skills in our energy exchange."

"And to think I only got hiccups," I said.

"I would imagine you gained a little more than that, if you only looked."

"Speaking of looking... what exactly are you searching for?"

"What do you think I'm searching for?" she replied.

"Traces of intruders, I suppose. Oscar Knight in particular."

She nodded. "And finding none, fortunately. I don't think he broke through my spells. I did layer them up well."

"Using Maisie's botanicals? Including the rangleroot?"

"Yes, indeed. It's a very handy plant but doesn't last, unfortunately. Someone should genetically modify it for stamina."

"Maisie probably would have if it could be done."

I watched as she scanned Mom's treasured oak buffet, which had been handed down for generations. Liberty had as good a claim to it, if not better.

At about the midway point, her fingers started to glow. It was subtle. Just a slight golden tinge that seemed to trail up her arm and into her chest.

"Did you see that, Bixby?" I asked, silently.

"Saw it and felt it," he said. "Can you do it?"

When Liberty moved on to the china cabinet, I sat down on one of the dining room chairs. It felt more comfortable than it technically was, simply from familiarity. "All good?" I asked her.

"So far. I'm going to run up to the bedrooms and scan fully. You can join me if you like."

"I'll just chill out here. It's been a busy day and I'll tell you all about it over Ren's famous omelets."

"Omelets. Really." She sounded as snooty as a queen, and her disgust was enough to propel her out of the room with Harold, leaving me alone with Bixby and the family furniture.

"All hands on deck," Bixby said, his chuckle full of extra delight.

I wasted no time getting out of the chair and letting my finger-tips dangle over the buffet. Starting at the same end she did, I moved slowly along, trying to register any changes in energy.

Sure enough, at the midpoint, a tingling began. As I watched, a golden light traveled from my fingertips and up my forearm. A bubble of heat filled my chest.

"What's in there?" Bixby asked.

"Treasure of some sort," I said. "There's a drawer inside where Gran kept the sterling flatware."

I bent to open the door and found it locked. More than locked. The tingling stopped and another feeling began. Vague menace.

"She's spelled it," Bixby said.

"Up to the hilt," I said. "We're not going to get to the rangleroot the easy way."

He cocked his head and stared at me. "Well, then... What's the hard way?"

CHAPTER TWENTY-THREE

"Groveling," Liberty answered from behind us. "Better yet, bribery."

We turned to find her in the doorway, arms crossed. She'd hadn't gone upstairs, after all. It was probably a test to see if I'd studied her demonstration and learned from it.

"I don't appreciate you poking around my things," she said, frowning.

"Technically, this dining room set belongs to me, too. It's part of the Brighton collection."

"Weasel words, from a weaselly witch and her canine weasel."

"Excuse me," Mr. Bixby said, aloud. "You're the sneak who said she didn't have rangleroot. You lied outright to Janelle. All she did was run her hands around and check your story. You're defensive because it didn't check out."

Harold sent a little gust in Bixby's direction, blowing the dog into the buffet. I shook my head at the Aussie and bent to pick up my dachshund. "It's okay, Bixby. Time to move on to plan B."

"No groveling," he said. "It's unseemly, especially with someone who stole nearly all your powers and left you with nothing more than flowery hiccups."

Liberty stepped into the room, still frowning. "Not true. That energy work came directly from me. Have you ever done something like that before, Janelle?"

"Similar but different," I said. "This was far more efficient. I could see and smell the plants, and even tell the difference between what you took from various gardens, including Sonia's and Arnold's. There are markers."

She looked moderately impressed. "What else?"

"I can tell there's a big bundle of rangleroot. You can definitely spare enough to protect all the dogs, including Octavia's."

"It is a big bundle and it was even bigger. It doesn't keep, you see, and most spells call for a lot of it." Strolling around the room, she added, "Plus, as you know, it's dreadfully hard to grow. So, the answer is no, Janelle."

"Is this where you grovel?" Bixby asked, out loud. "Do you even know how?"

"She doesn't," Liberty answered for me. "Groveling isn't in the Brighton collection."

I laughed. "I'm capable. For a good cause. A dog's safety comes under that category."

"No need to waste your dignity," my cousin said. "I've already protected the dogs and your stores, and since it needs to be refreshed often, I can't spare any for the Knights."

"But I promised Octavia..." It came out as a whine, which was close to groveling.

"You promised something you didn't have, which is never a good strategy." Finally, Liberty perched on the edge of a chair. "Don't underestimate Oscar's resourcefulness, Janelle. He can get his hands on anything he needs far more easily than I can. He has connections, whereas many of mine have..."

Her voice drifted off and Bixby happily jumped in. "Died. I thought you embraced that word, Liberty. That's what you said."

Her lips puckered. "So I did. My recovery has changed a few

things. The further I go, the more I want to live. The word doesn't come as easily anymore."

I sat down too, facing her. "Cousin Liberty, we could go round and round, here. I could grovel and maybe even offer a bribe. But instead I'm just going to remind you that we're family and sometimes we need to make sacrifices. I feel a little tacky reminding you that I already made a pretty big one for you that nearly killed me."

Mr. Bixby laughed in delight. "Ah, good one Janelle. Go straight for the guilt card."

"Be quiet, weasel dog." Liberty started to put her elbows on the table and changed her mind. "I don't respond well to guilt. Or the family duty card, to be honest. You *chose* to help free me from Oscar's spell. I choose not to help him or his family."

"I did choose freely but I had no idea what it would cost me," I said. "Or that magical hiccups came with the deal."

She threw herself back in the chair. "I don't like to be shackled by obligation."

"Fair enough, but if you'd been more connected to family and community, chances are you wouldn't have been stuck in here for thirty years."

Getting up again, she paced. "At the risk of inflating your ego even more, no one else could have gotten me out of here. Oscar knows that, and it's going to be our biggest challenge. Rule number one of warfare is know thy enemy, Janelle. What's his greatest weakness?"

"Octavia," Bixby answered for me.

Leaning back, I shook my head. "I won't sacrifice Tavi in this battle. We have a code of ethics."

"We?" she asked. "As in the Brightons?"

"We, as in Bixby and me. I was on the run for years—the underdog—and no one gave me the benefit of the doubt except Gran, Renata, and then Sinda. So now, I make sure I do that for others, including Octavia."

"And Oscar? Because they're a package deal."

I thought about it and instead of answering, waggled my eyebrows. "How about a wager? If I can break into the buffet and get the rangleroot, you let me take enough for Octavia for two weeks. That should get everyone through Thanksgiving and Maisie's murder investigation. We'll reassess then."

She moved back into the doorway. Framed by the light from the kitchen, she was an impressive woman. A warrior. And of course, she couldn't go down without a fight.

"You'll find out soon enough that it's every witch for herself in this town, regardless of family. Tavi has what it takes but she's chosen to be delicate."

"And that's put Oscar on the offensive all the time. He can't ever pass up a fight in case she's hurt."

"So our deal is that you get two weeks to help Tavi get on track to take care of herself, whatever that means. Further, we all need to be resourceful, so I won't keep supplying you with rangleroot even to protect your own dogs."

"Fine," I said.

"Fine," she said. "Then take it if you can."

I sighed. "You mean I still have to break into the buffet?"

"Of course." She actually clasped her hands in girlish excitement. "Show me what you've got, girl."

Standing, I turned to face the buffet, running my fingers across it like before. Once I hit the sweet spot, and energy flowed into my fingers, I closed my eyes and looked inward for clues. What kind of spell—or web of spells—had she cast on this piece to keep people out?

Words began to form on a mental screen in my mind. Plenty of them. A veritable scroll of spells unfurled.

Four of them, and all deceptively simple.

Now, all I had to do was reverse them. Trying the strategy she'd handed to me with her beginner's spell book was as good a place to start as any.

Pressing my lips closed, I silently read the first one backward. I had learned before that sounding out the syllables aloud could very much backfire. This time I just tried to capture the letters, the general sense of the non-word. Unsaying what had been said.

As I finished the first, my fingers felt something like a click and one magical lock opened. So I went on with the second, and then the third. The last one was a complicated mental mouthful and I worked through it slowly.

Only when the final spell unlocked did I dare open my eyes. When I did, Liberty's expression of mingled fury and shock made me hiccup. Sunflowers were cropping up somewhere but I couldn't see them.

Leaning over, I opened the buffet, and big, showy blooms spilled out.

"Get those stupid weeds away from my rangleroot," she said, elbowing me out of the way. "How did you do that, Janelle Brighton?"

"Hiccup?" I asked, deliberately misunderstanding her. "The bigger question is how do I not?"

She pulled out handfuls of sunflowers and threw them on the floor. "You will tell me how you broke my spells right now."

"Only if you tell me how to stop hiccupping."

Finally, she handed me a pot containing innocuous-looking plants already starting to droop. "I told you how. Grow your confidence like you would any plant and the hiccups will gradually fade away." She kicked at the sunflowers so that she didn't crush them underfoot. "Your turn."

"I read your mind, Cousin Liberty. And then I applied the lesson from your primer and reversed the spells."

"Liar." The word came not from Liberty and not even from

Bixby. Harold tilted his head to one side and wriggled his tailless butt in the sheepdog equivalent of a smile.

I smiled, too. The spells were very much in Liberty's mind but harder to access than Harold's, at least for me. He had witnessed her casting the spells and our connection fed them back to me with ease.

"Thank you," I told Harold, over our private line. "I want to try negotiation with the Knights before warfare."

"I know," he said. "We have the same goals. To keep everyone safe."

Liberty was preoccupied with the technique I'd shared. "Can I do that, too? Read other witches' minds and break their spells?"

"Possibly," I said. "But first you need to grow in confidence."

We all laughed. If there was one thing Liberty had in spades, it was confidence.

Renata appeared in the doorway carrying plates and cutlery. "Dinner's ready. What did I miss?"

"Family games night," Mr. Bixby said, stepping over the sunflowers. "Consider yourself lucky."

CHAPTER TWENTY-FOUR

The Beanstalk Café wasn't even open when I arrived the next morning, but Old Man Crossword was already there.

"Is he homeless?" I said, trying the door and finding it locked. "Does Valerie let him stay overnight?"

She came to the door, flipped the sign to open, and let me in. "Good morning, you two." She added in a whisper, "I wish I could say you were my first customers."

At least the guy bought a coffee. Steam wafted gently from his mug as he leaned in toward the newspaper, which was already spread out in front of him.

I placed my order and studiously ignored him as I walked to my usual table. He studiously ignored me back.

"You can feel that?" Bixby asked.

"Sure. It's like a dark cloud." I set the dog down on a chair. "Some people just can't take a good wiener joke."

"I'm one of those people. Although I enjoy it well enough when it's flung at someone else." He stared over at the man. "You sure it isn't because you ruined the crossword for him? I'm seeing letters flying around."

I closed my eyes for a second. "You're right. I see them, too."

Bixby laughed. "Of course you do. I only see them because you see them. And this is new."

Shrugging off my coat, I tossed it onto the bench beside him. "I suppose. I always felt things but I didn't see it in writing. Could come in handy."

As I walked back to the counter to collect my coffee, I muttered, "Salutations. Thirty-three across."

Mr. Crossword looked up at me and scowled. I was surprised to see his eyes were bright blue behind tinted lenses.

Sitting down, I found Bixby staring at me and asked, "What?"

"You'd give me a hard time for doing that. You wrecked the guy's day for nothing."

"I didn't wreck his day. In fact, I made it better with a bum lead. He could have hours of fun and challenge trying to find the right word."

The dog laughed. "Still. You told Liberty we had a code. To give people the benefit of the doubt. Was this totally in line with our principles?"

I took a sip of coffee and regretted it instantly after scalding my lip. "Maybe not. I guess it was a jerk move. I'm crabby today."

"Because the police canceled the restaurant's grand opening, I suppose. Don't really blame you as we were all looking forward to it. Ethan promised Bijou and me foie gras."

"That's a little rich, isn't it? Even for a special occasion?"

"Not at all," he said, accepting the bit of biscotti I offered him. "I have the heart of a hero, thanks to you. It won't plug up with fancy French treats."

I took a bite of the biscotti and sighed. It was dry and virtually flavorless. Once Renata's bakery was open, she could supply Valerie with something more palatable than bran bombs and boring biscuits.

Fortunately, I hadn't come for the baked goods. My morning visit was to check in on Atticus and see if Octavia might come by. We hadn't exchanged contact information so I had no way to let her know I had the rangleroot. I certainly wasn't going to drop by the Knight house. It was in the ritzy part of town, where people had pools and pool houses. Jared had rubbed that in thoroughly in high school. Living in an old manor with a ghost—or at least rumors of one—hadn't done much for my popularity.

"I thought we moved past all that angst," Mr. Bixby said, eyeing the rest of the biscotti. "Isn't there a statute of limitations for these things?"

"Teen angst probably lives forever, but I hope not." My spirits lifted as Atticus sauntered out of the back room, white tail fanning a friendly greeting. "Hey, buddy."

The last part was silent because of Mr. Crossword, but he seemed to be fully focused on his puzzle. So much so that he jumped when Atticus pulled a book from the shelf and it hit the floor with a thud. I started to get up to put it back but before I could, a cool breeze hit me and someone came into the café.

I barely had time to register the scarf and sunglasses before Octavia Knight pulled out the chair opposite me and sank into it. "You have it?" she asked, reaching across to take my hands.

Leaning back was an automatic response. I had been avoiding unsolicited impressions from others for at least as long as I'd had teen angst. "Good morning," I said, softening the reaction. "How did you know?"

She let the glasses slide down and stared at me blankly. "I'm not sure. It just struck me when I woke up that I should drive over." Her impeccable lipstick framed a smile. "I must be right."

I leaned forward again. "Let's be discreet, Tavi. We have company."

Glancing around, she smiled. "Norris Strump? Don't worry about him. He's a lovely man. A former town clerk and librarian. I'd introduce you but he's very serious about his crossword puzzle. Every day he competes with himself and keeps notes. I daresay there's no one in town with a better vocabulary."

"Interesting," I said, pointing to Atticus' handiwork. "This is quite the literary café. Books keep bursting off the shelf."

She got up, collected the two hardcover volumes and examined them. "*Gone with the Wind* and *Wuthering Heights*. Two old favorites. When I was young, I adored tragic love stories." Pushing them to one side of the table, she sighed. "Now that I'm caught up in one, I prefer something lighter."

Mr. Bixby put his paws on my leg, stared over the edge of the table at her and said, "Get over yourself, lady. There's quite enough angst here without yours."

"How adorable," she said. "It's like he's talking to me."

"He is adorable. Pushy, but adorable." I moved his paws off the table and took his hint. "Mrs. Knight. Tavi. I do have what you need but before I give it to you I need to ask for something in return."

Her smiled faded. "Of course. I only hope I can deliver."

"You can. That's exactly what I want you to do. Deliver something to Oscar."

She brightened again. "Sure. I'll leave it outside the pool house."

"Does he still make tea for you every morning?"

"Not today," she said. "Or yesterday, actually."

It was the confirmation I needed. He was out of rangleroot and she was unprotected.

"How do you feel about that?" I asked.

Taking her glasses off, she stared up at the ceiling. "Honestly, Janelle, I don't feel quite right. Perhaps he's moving on and that's given me second thoughts." Her fingers folded and refolded on the table. "Maybe I'm not quite ready for it to be over."

I couldn't help smiling. "I hoped you'd say that, because I ran into Oscar yesterday and it was clear to me how much he adores you."

"Really? What did he say?"

"I wish I could tell you he said flowery things but he wasn't his usual suave self. I'd almost say he was sick with despair." Pulling a small dark bottle out of my purse, I pushed it across the table. "I made him a tonic that will put some pep in his step."

She took it in her hands. "You want me to slip my husband a tonic?"

"Better yet, make a tea out of it. He'll see it as a romantic gesture and you'll kill two birds with one stone."

Mr. Bixby cleared his throat conspicuously. "Care to rephrase that?"

"Janelle, I can't just randomly serve my husband a tonic. Especially from someone he's been in conflict with before."

Reaching out, I folded her fingers around the little bottle. "What do you feel?"

She tried to pull away, flustered. "Nothing. I feel nothing."

"Try harder," I said. "Does an image come to mind? A sound? A smell?"

Blinking rapidly, she squeezed the bottle. "I see a waterfall with a whirlpool at the bottom." She leaned back. "A geyser. With steam."

"Healing springs," I said. "What else?"

She tipped her head and then smiled. "A field of sunflowers."

I nodded. "I'm here to tell you that your mother was wrong. Your husband was wrong. Everyone who ever said you lacked magical ability was wrong."

"But I'm a—a dud, as they call it now. Everyone said so."

"Not me. So I'm telling you to trust your instincts. And if you find you agree with me when you get home, serve your husband a nice cup of tea and see if it doesn't reignite something."

I touched her hand again and she jumped. "Oooh. I felt a little spark there."

"That's a very good start. Not that I'm qualified to be a marriage counselor. I haven't had a date in forever."

"Perhaps sparks will fly for you, tonight," she said. "At the opening of Chez Bogart. It's the Wyldwood event of the season."

"Canceled," I said. "Ethan let us know last night that the police put the kibosh on it, because there's been no arrest in the case of Maisie Gledhill."

Slipping the vial into her purse, she frowned. "If life stopped every time... well, a life stopped in Wyldwood, nothing would get done. I'll speak to Ruthann Longmuir."

I held up my palm. "The mayor must have been involved in the decision. Let's not trouble her. The party will happen another night."

"I suppose." She ran her hand over the books. "I just feel like celebrating. And you haven't even given me the rangleroot, yet."

Taking the hint, I slid the package across the table to her. "I hear it doesn't last long or keep well, so bear that in mind, Tavi. We'll need to find another source in two weeks."

"I understand." Touching the package, she caught my eye. "Do you think I have what it takes to do this myself, or should I wait for you?"

"I'd be happy to help if you need it. Give it some thought." I gestured around. "You know where to find me."

She pushed the chair back. "I do. And you're rapidly becoming the daughter I never had."

Mr. Bixby laughed and I avoided a shudder by focusing on my burnt lip. "That's so kind of you to say."

"I always wanted more children but Oscar insisted one was enough."

When that one was Jared, I'd have called it quits, too. "You have Philomena. She's the girl you need."

"My first female dog, actually. Till now, I've always had boys. A different breed every time." She sighed. "Oscar never liked any of them, but especially the English setter. He's a little fonder of Phillie."

"Well now," Bixby said, standing up to tap the books. "A plot twist if ever I heard one."

"An English setter?" I asked. "That's an uncommon breed."

"More common then. It's been about twenty years since my sweet Atticus passed. I just adored him but Oscar called him a clown."

Atticus the ghost responded to that by tossing another book on the floor. His mouth hung open in a goofy pant but there was something about his expression that told me this dog was no clown when it came to heart. "Was Atticus protective of you?"

"Very much so, and I think Oscar was a little jealous."

"And did Atticus live a good long life?"

"He did, but it wasn't the life I wished for him. He deserved more fun than Oscar would let him have. I often thought I should place him with another family."

"Oscar?" Bixby suggested. "That would have been the right choice."

"Atticus, I mean," Octavia said, although I knew she couldn't hear Bixby. "I wanted him to live his best life, but I was too selfish to part with him. If I could do it over..."

"You'd give up the dog?" I asked.

She shook her head and winked. "I'd give up the husband. Now I've learned to put the dog first and everything else will fall into place."

Slipping her glasses back on, she gathered her things. "I named Atticus after a character in one of my favorite books, you know."

"*To Kill a Mockingbird*, I expect."

"That's right." She squeezed my shoulder, sending a cascade of warmth and gratitude into my heart, and then headed for the door. "Bye, now."

"Bye, Tavi."

Another voice overlapped with mine. It didn't belong to Bixby, Atticus or even Valerie.

Norris Strump looked surprised that the words had come out of his mouth, and doubled down on his puzzle before it could happen again.

CHAPTER TWENTY-FIVE

The grand opening of Chez Bogart was back on. I didn't know if Octavia had pulled some strings or the two police chiefs had relented. But as soon as Whimsy closed for the evening, I rushed home to get ready with Ren.

It was the most fun we'd had since high school. Ren hadn't moved her full wardrobe into the manor, so we carried my party gear into Mom's dressing room and went all in. With all the events I'd had to attend while working in resorts, there were lots of options.

Bijou sat on the bed meant for Sir Nigel, dodging the castoffs we fired her way and enjoying the girlish fun. Bixby, on the other hand, sprawled on the floor deliberately trying to trip us.

"This giddiness is unseemly," he said. "You do remember that someone was murdered two days ago, and that Liberty is still considered a suspect? And possibly the two of you."

"If we were suspects, Drew would have brought us in for questioning by now," I said. "Can't we just take a little break from stress for an hour, Bixby? We'll be on duty all night."

He rolled out of the way. "Fine. As long as you're not planning to spend the night flirting."

"Ren can spend the night flirting, while you and I work the

room," I said. "I doubt any of the suspects will be there, but we might get to chat with their friends and neighbors."

Spinning to check every angle in Mom's three-way mirror, Ren came down in favor of a bold red strapless gown. "What do you think?"

"Great choice. It screams 'wallflower no more,'" I said.

Bixby snorted. "More like 'pick me out of the crowd and take me down first.'"

"Shut up, short stuff," Bijou said. "This is a big night for Renny-ren and she deserves it."

Ren walked over and patted her dog. "Thanks for the vote of support. But this is Ethan's big night and I doubt he'll have much time to talk to us. My big moment comes next week when Flour Girl opens. After that, we can probably all relax a little. Presuming the killer is behind bars."

"I'm sure the police will figure it out by then," I said. "So far, I'm stumped."

Bixby stood up and swaggered over to the bed. "Maybe if you weren't playing matchmaker with Octavia and Oscar you'd have more time for the real work. I don't get why you're taking such an interest in the Knights' relationship problems."

"You know why," I said, holding up two of my favorite black dresses. They were very similar, but one had pockets and more flare in the skirt. I hated to admit it but things like that were selling points now. Pockets meant my hands could be free to juggle a dog. And a flirty skirt meant there was room to run. "Atticus turned up the day Maisie died. There's got to be a reason for that. He was Octavia's dog but I don't think he wants to go back to her. So there's more to his story. Besides, a happy Oscar is better than a miserable one."

"I don't know about that," Bixby said. "He was happy the first two times he tried to kill you in Wyldwood. And when he had you chased out of town. Plus down south." He cocked his head. "Am I forgetting anything?"

"It could always be worse," I said. "And there's the possibility of making things better."

"By bringing back a dog he hated more than the rest?" he pressed.

"Bixby." The voice was curt. "You leave Witchy alone."

My dog glared at her. "Don't use that tone with me, poodle. It's my job to keep Janelle alive, and that means questioning her decisions and redirecting her when she falls into some romantic vortex."

"He's right, Bijou," I said. "About questioning my thinking. Not about the romantic vortex." I nudged the dachshund with my bare foot. "All I'd ask is that you remember some of this happens beyond conscious thought."

A dismissive grunt was all I got for my protests. "Maybe the last ten percent. Even less. Most sleuthing is old-fashioned brain to grindstone."

"It makes my head hurt," Ren said, slipping on shoes. "And what's with the books Atticus keeps tossing?"

"Good question, and I intend to ask him tomorrow." I slipped into the flared dress, touched up my makeup quickly and rearranged my curls.

A few minutes later we walked into the kitchen and found Sinda looking like a million bucks in a shimmery blue dress and jacket. Just two months ago she'd looked like a timid woman and now she rivaled Liberty for pizazz.

"You're gorgeous, girls," she said, slipping her arms into her coat. "May this evening bring you the romance you well deserve."

I considered taking a cab into town but decided against it for the same practical reasons as the flared dress. If I had to make a quick getaway, I wanted my own wheels.

"I'm glad you still have your wits about you," Bixby said, as I carried him into the already crowded restaurant. I had expected complaints from the dog about his black and silver bowtie, but instead I caught him angling his head to catch his reflection in the restaurant windows.

"You're dashing, my friend," I said. "And that's the last time we speak aloud until we're back in the car. Got it?"

"You're the one who's always forgetting," he said, still out loud. "I demand to be carried the entire night, by the way. The place is packed and I don't intend to depart my current life as a stiletto fatality."

"A sit-down dinner would have been better for the dogs," Ren said. "But there was so much interest I can't blame Ethan for going with cocktails and finger foods."

"Easier to mingle." I peered around as we hung our coats on the rack near the door. "Sonia Dinogue is here. I've got a few more questions for her."

"I didn't expect to see Trina and Brianna Peck," Ren said. "Brianna still looks utterly miserable."

"That's because some blockhead has a pincher on her arm," Bixby said. "Looks like someone who'd call himself Bucky."

"Could be his given name," Sinda said. "It happens."

Brianna's fiancé wasn't unattractive, per se, but he was large, dark and square, and gave off a negative vibe that felt out of place in the quaint bistro.

"Janny, look," Ren whispered. "Your efforts are working."

I turned to see Oscar Knight and his wife standing near the open patio doors talking to Ethan. When Oscar draped his arm over Tavi's shoulders, she bent her knees and eased out from under it. My work clearly wasn't over.

"Incoming," Bixby said. "Tavi's seen you and she's making a beeline for the matchmaker."

I tried slipping into the crowd but it was so dense I got stuck. Octavia was beaming and beautiful in a silver dress and her husband was hard on her heels. "Janny, darling!" she said. "I'm so glad the mayor decided to let the party go ahead. We have Oscar to thank for working his charm."

Oscar looked like there might be more charm at his disposal than yesterday, when he was weaving down Liberty's street. He seemed about half as menacing as his normal state, which was about right for the dose of antidote I'd sent.

Bijou and Bixby both sniffed him blatantly and he reared back. "Excuse me. This is one of my best jackets. It was all I could do to keep Philomena off me before we left. Why don't we get a non-shedding dog, Tavi?"

"You know I'd love a second, Oscar." She winked at me blatantly. "Maybe Janelle can hook me up. She always seems to be surrounded by dogs."

"It's my fate, and I couldn't have chosen a better one," I said, hugging Bixby till he gave a fake wheeze. "What breed would you choose, Oscar?"

"Honestly, I could do without pets, period." He caught his wife's eye and added, "But I can't do without my Tavi, so whatever she thinks is best."

I accepted a flute of champagne from a waiter and used the opportunity to slip away into the crowd.

The ploy didn't work. Within seconds, a hand landed on my bare arm and snakes coiled in both directions. I thought about shaking it off, but instead touched Oscar's watch. Its tiny gemstones confirmed the dogs' noses and my own intuition. "It's good to see you looking a little better, Oscar. You're shaking off whatever ailed you."

"Just a cold," he said. "My wife made me some herbal tea and it brought me around pretty quickly."

"Don't ask about the pipes," Bixby said, on our private channel. "You can tell by the way he's mincing around that it wasn't his best afternoon."

I decided to pinch the chatline closed. Distractions were

never good when Oscar was around, but particularly when he was holding my arm. At least I didn't feel faint, which had happened the first time he was in such close proximity. That was either because I was a little stronger or he was a little weaker... or both.

"I want to ask you something," he said, "and be honest because I will know."

"Not necessarily," Bixby said, forcing himself past my mental barricade. "Janelle, I refuse to be silenced when a serpent is actually touching you."

"You can ask, Oscar," I said. "But you'll need to let go of my arm."

He stared at his hand as if it belonged to someone else. "Of course. I'm sorry."

I still had to help his fingers release by mentally repelling them one by one. Oscar certainly wasn't operating at full capacity.

When I could back away, I met his eyes. "What would you like to know?"

I expected him to ask about the tea, or the rangleroot, or perhaps my clandestine meetings with his wife. So what he said next surprised me. "Do you really have my wife's rings?"

There was no point evading him. He probably had a tracking spell on them.

"Yes. She asked me to hold onto them for her, Oscar. They're safe and I'm eager to return them."

"But why? You're the last person who should be holding her rings."

"In your opinion. I guess Tavi thinks differently. This wasn't something I wanted, Oscar, trust me. I agree that it's best not to come between you two and I've felt anxious about it."

"Then give them back."

"I will, and this time she might take them. She seemed to feel uncomfortable around you. I don't know the details."

His silver-gray eyes blinked a few times. "She felt uncomfortable with me."

It was a statement, not a question, but I answered anyway. "That's how I interpreted it. But I know how much she means to you and obviously you're convincing her, too. She's here with you tonight."

"I always take care of her." His normally brusque voice nearly cracked. "What was she thinking?"

"Oscar, talk to her, please. As you said, there's precious little room between a man and his wife. Now *I'm* uncomfortable."

"You heard the girl, Oscar. Step away from Janelle this instant."

I had never been so happy to see Liberty. She was a tall woman and her heels brought her nearly to eye level with Oscar. Her fierce green glare forced him back a little and her personality did the rest.

"And now you can tell me why you were loitering in my yard last night," she said. "My cameras caught you weaving down the street like a common drunk."

He rallied quickly and offered a small smile. "I just wanted to stop by and apologize to you. I'm glad you're—uh—back."

"You mean *alive*." Liberty looked skeptical. "You're saying you came by to congratulate me on surviving the spell you cast with your posse of— Oh, hello, Arnold. You're here, too. What a reunion."

A man who was a good 10 years older and 40 pounds heavier than Oscar stepped into our midst. "Liberty, you look well," he said. "Time's been kind to you."

I shook my head slightly. Arnold was baiting her and Liberty normally had little in the way of willpower.

"You wouldn't either if you'd lived her life," Bixby said. "I've taken a peek inside. Since she stole your power, I've got easier access."

"Then tell her not to take the bait," I said. "Harold isn't here to do it."

"Where is the furry cyclone?" Bixby looked down and around. "It's not like I have so much time on my paws that I can support both of you."

Nonetheless, he stepped up to the plate. Leaning out of my arms, he tapped Liberty's wrist. "I'd like you to carry me now," he said, silently. "You're the Brighton matriarch in what is turning into a rather difficult situation."

I don't know that she understood his words but the tap did the trick. She held out her hands and accepted the dachshund. It calmed her immediately and she gave Arnold a stiff smile. "Thank you, Arnold. Modern cosmetics make a world of difference. I hope you and Oscar aren't too macho to try them."

I glanced over and saw Drew speaking to Ethan. Both men caught my eye, and then Ethan sent a couple of waiters our way with canapes. I sent a smile back, grateful for Drew's support and wishing I had my dog in my arms.

"You've got me, Witchy. Not too big to carry."

Bending, I whispered, "Thank you, Bijou. Is Ren safe?"

"I asked her to stay with Sinda till this is over."

"Till what's over?" I asked.

"I don't know yet. But something doesn't smell too good."

Oscar's ruby ring appeared in front of my face. "Do you need a hand, young lady? You've been down there a while."

"Absolutely fine." I lifted Bijou, who was nearly three times Bixby's weight but somehow seemed lighter. "I just never feel quite right without a dog in my arms."

"Family failing," Liberty said, giving Bixby a squeeze that was probably calibrated for an Aussie. This time his wheeze was legit. "Perhaps this is the right moment for the Brighton ladies to powder our noses." She winked at me. "Is that still a thing?"

"Very much so. Let's go and freshen up."

"Any fresher and you'd be twins," Arnold said.

Liberty tried to ease away. "Flattery will get you everywhere."

Arnold's smile turned as feral as Oscar's used to be. "Into your botanicals, perhaps? I have it on good authority that you've got a supply of rangleroot on hand. It's a very difficult plant to grow. Whoever dispatched Maisie wasn't aware of her unique skillset, I presume."

"I certainly know the value of both rangleroot and someone with a green thumb," she said. "Some of us will need to find a new supplier. I was hoping you gentlemen could provide me with a connection. It's the least you could do, considering."

"Considering what?" Arnold said.

Bixby squirmed in Liberty's arms and gave her a stern lecture that seemed to roll off her. "Considering you did your very best to kill me, Arnold. I should think that would give me access to all the best plants for years to come."

He pressed his lips together and color crept up around his overly tight collar. "Oscar, I'm quite sure you said you detected rangleroot at Liberty's house."

Oscar stared at his friend blankly. "I don't recall saying that. Liberty wasn't at home and I didn't stay."

"You gentlemen both need a snack," I said. "And luckily, Chef Ethan has sent in the troops."

Ronna Tweeze and Mike Spenser, former staff at the Beanstalk Café, were dressed in crisp white shirts and black pants. They both smiled as they offered their trays not to the seniors in our midst, but me.

"Try the foie gras," Ronna said, twirling the silver tray.

"Or a croquette," Mike said, with a flirty smile that made color heat up my own cheeks. The young man thought I'd hit on him once and might do it again.

I adjusted Bijou under my arm and pondered how to manage a drink, a dog and a canapé.

"Skip it," Bixby said, either to Liberty, me or both.

Arnold didn't wait for me to decline, shoving me aside to serve himself. He scooped up foie gras with one hand and a couple of croquettes with the other. Popping them all into his mouth, he smirked as he chewed.

I set my glass on Mike's tray and reached for a croquette.

"Witchy, stop." Bijou leaned out of my arms and sniffed loudly. "Stop! It's poison."

"Watch the dog," Oscar said. "Don't let her touch the—"

"Poison," I said. And then louder, "Poison!"

CHAPTER TWENTY-SIX

The next few moments were a whirlwind. Literally.

Harold dashed into view, circled all of us and sent the finger foods spiraling into the air. Then everything seemed to slow down, and even drop into slow motion, as Arnold fell to the floor, clutching his throat with one hand and his belly with the other.

Dragging my eyes away, I saw Drew pushing through the crowd toward us with Ethan in his wake. Even in the hubbub, I could tell our friend the chef believed his new business was going down in flames.

Ronna and Mike stood frozen, at first, but as the crowd surged forward, they were absorbed into it.

Harold herded Liberty out of the fray and she clutched Bixby to her chest. My heart was in my throat and I desperately wanted my dog. In a second, however, Harold was back and deftly steering me away from Arnold's prone form. "Go," the Aussie said. "Take the poodle into the kitchen and find the poison."

I did exactly as he said and sent a message to Bixby: create a distraction.

"There's not enough going on for you?" my dog said.

Tavi Knight ran to Oscar's side and he held her back with

arms spread wide. Arnold was thrashing and groaning at Oscar's feet. There was a chance he could recover, but perhaps not through the aid of the sirens in the distance. It was highly likely the poison was a magical concoction that could only be remedied by people like Oscar and Liberty—if, indeed, they wanted it remedied.

Bijou struggled to be set down. I did as she wished and then followed her into the kitchen. We might only have a few minutes before the paramedics took Arnold away and Drew's colleagues swarmed through Ethan's new restaurant.

In the doorway to the alley, Ronna and Mike stood clutching each other and whispering. I could sense easily that they were deciding whether or not to run.

Hurrying over, I grabbed each of them by the hand. "Do you know who had access to the foie gras? The croquettes?"

"Everyone," Ronna said. The blue eyeshadow from her days serving at the Beanstalk had been upgraded to something subtler, but mascara was streaming down her cheeks. "Ethan did tours of the kitchen before you got here. Nearly everyone's been through. Even Arnold Blatchford."

"Did anyone touch the food?" I asked.

Mike shrugged. "Seemed like nearly everyone bent over to sniff."

He glanced at Ronna and she nodded. Then she smoothed her apron and went back out into the dining room.

"I wonder if it was just one tray." I turned to the counters and stove, and found my canine poison detector standing on her hind legs, sniffing.

"This one," she said. "This one, this one."

Peering into a large pot on the stove, I saw the remnants of mashed potatoes. The troublemaker was the croquettes.

I sent her a silent message. "Can you tell what poison it is?"

"No," she said. "Get the little sausage. He knows his plants."

There was an indignant snort in my head. "Tell that silly poodle to stand down. I'm on my way."

A yelp in the dining room came not from the dogs but from Liberty as Mr. Bixby freed himself. Seconds later the kitchen door cracked open and he trotted in, nose already high.

"Gillseed," he said. "Very rare. Never smelled it in Wyldwood before."

I sighed. That took us no closer to the truth.

"Harold?" I mentally reached out for the Aussie. "Could you please tell Liberty it's gillseed and see if she knows what to do?"

"Hopefully Liberty wasn't the one who poisoned Arnold." Bixby sounded quite cheerful. "Maybe she was hoping to take him out with Oscar in one fell swoop."

"She wouldn't have put me in danger," I said. "I was going straight for the croquette when Arnold went down."

"Takes very little. One of the faster toxins. Obviously."

Harold's hoarse voice entered my mind. "Done. Liberty's misleading the paramedics."

I turned to find Mike Spenser staring at me. "Looks like you're still struggling with rumination, Janelle. It's not too late to join our self-development study group."

"Thanks, Mike." I smiled back, trying to keep it neutral so as not to mislead him. Even if he weren't a decade younger than me, I'd never be interested. My heart belonged to Drew, even if we could never do anything about it.

"I'm serious," he said. "A year ago something like this would have rattled me. The police will investigate me and I have a bit of a checkered past. Instead, I'm just focusing on my breathing." Resting one hand on his aproned diaphragm, he pulled in a long breath through his nose. "In for six, out for eight, hold for twelve. That's my secret code."

"I appreciate your letting me in on the secret, Mike. I promise I'll give that a try."

"Good for what ails you. Except poison, I suppose."

"Poor Ethan," I said. "It's hard enough to make a go of a new restaurant without something like this happening. The sooner the truth comes out, the better. Are you sure you didn't see anything strange?"

Mike stepped out of the open door and into the alley, and I followed with both dogs. "The Gledhill clan was bickering," he said. "I don't know why they'd socialize so soon after what happened to Maisie. Brianna's fiancé had the nerve to tell Ethan to add more salt to the artichoke dip. Biggest insult to a trained chef."

"Bucky, right?" I said. "I heard he had an edge."

"Bucky Mulhairn, yeah. Big guy. He pulled Brianna out here and they were arguing. More like, he was arguing. She didn't say much."

"Did you pick up anything specific?"

He shook his head. "I was running around. Trying to make the party go well for Ethan."

"Ahem." Mr. Bixby jumped into my interrogation, at least on the inside. "At the risk of encouraging inappropriate touching... let's try some touching."

"Are you kidding?" I asked the dog. "You know what happened last time."

As it turned out, the same thing happened this time.

A strong wind hit me from behind and I stumbled forward into Mike Spenser. My hands came up to brace for impact and landed haphazardly.

"Chesticle," Bixby said. "Right chesticle, Janelle. If you're going to take liberties, make it count."

I moved my hand and connected with the spot Mike's stud had been a few weeks ago. There was no telling if it would still be there, as he was trying to start over with a new image.

The tiny topaz chip I hadn't seen was still transmitting like a beacon. The information Mike was too busy and distracted to register from his surroundings had still been logged and filed. Bucky's raised voice had made the waiter uncomfortable.

The young couple had been arguing about Sonia Dinogue's offer to buy Maisie's property. Bucky was pressuring Brianna to accept it. He had bills to pay, and Brianna wouldn't get the wedding she wanted if she let this opportunity go by. It was too good to pass up, he said. But Brianna wasn't ready to give up on her grandmother's dream, even if Trina was willing. More offers would come at the right time, she said.

I pushed away from Mike but he held onto my hand and put it on his midriff. "Here. This is where to focus the breathing."

"Got it," I said. "Thank you so much, Mike."

Ren stuck her head out the back door. "Janelle, you'd better come. Harold's sent stuff flying and Liberty can't stop him."

"Won't stop him, you mean," I said, grabbing Bixby and following her. "She's enjoying the drama."

Mr. Bixby settled comfortably on my hip. "If you'd been on house arrest for decades, you'd enjoy a show, too," he said. "Trust me, I know."

CHAPTER TWENTY-SEVEN

After the police dispersed the crowd, I sent Sinda and Ren home with Liberty, hoping to have a private moment alone with Drew Gillock.

Mr. Bixby gave a sly chuckle. "Not *that* sort of moment," I said. "The sort of moment where I beat around the bush to let him know what I picked up from Mike. I need to figure out a way to suggest the police look into Bucky's history. There's something dark about that guy and I don't want to go near him unless I absolutely need to."

"You'll probably need to," Bixby said. "Hate to be a Debbie downer again, but you know how these things go."

I hung around for quite some time watching the police scour the restaurant, and when Ethan sat down alone in a corner, I went over to join him.

"The place is doomed," he said. "I'm doomed. I sunk every dollar and more into expanding and now I'm the chef who poisons people. It'll be all over the news."

"Getting news coverage has an upside," I said. "This will pass."

He shook his head. "Very few restaurants survive as it is."

"I know. But you already have a great reputation and had a fabulous turnout tonight." Sitting opposite him, I patted his arm. It was meant to be a friendly gesture, but then I realized Ethan might have a few useful impressions available. Thank goodness he was wearing a wristwatch to make snooping easier. "Despite what happened, you should be proud."

"I was. Why would people target me?"

"It was just a crime of opportunity," I said. "You know what this town is like."

He mused in silence, apparently unaware of my fingers on his watch.

Inside Ethan's mind, I found an embarrassment of riches. While he was circulating among his guests, he had delicately intervened on several conversations that verged on arguments. Oscar and Arnold. Oscar and Sonia. And Oscar again, this time with Liberty.

"Oscar, Oscar, Oscar," Bixby said, silently. "That's what happens when you give a man a remedy he doesn't deserve."

Ignoring him, I stuck with Ethan's memory, hoping to get a clue as to the nature of the disputes. The word I heard had puzzled Ethan, but not me.

Rangleroot.

Oscar was apparently hitting people up right, left and center to get his hands on it. Clearly his wife hadn't shared her private stash. Their reunion was still tenuous at best.

"Obviously, or she'd want her rings back," Bixby said.

Ethan had also noticed Sonia Dinogue talking to Bucky and then Trina and finally, Brianna. The images in Ethan's mind confirmed my impression that Bucky was little more than a thug. Brianna could do so much better than him.

"Less matchmaker, more sleuth," Bixby suggested. "Unless you want to make a plug for Renata while you're poking around Ethan's mental file cabinets."

I pulled my hand away from the watch quickly. One thing I did not want to do was meddle in Ren's love life, when most things I tried seemed to get worse before they got better.

"You're being too hard on yourself again," Bixby said. "It's not like there's a how-to for this life we're living. We do our best and that's all we can do."

I waited another few minutes to talk to Drew but he was on his knees beside James Barrow. They were examining the fallen tray of crushed croquettes under the bright police lights.

Finally I decided to call Drew later, and Bixby and I headed out to Elsa.

"Let's take a run by the Beanstalk Café on the way home," I said. "We might just make it before closing."

In fact, Valerie was sweeping the floor when we pulled up outside and the sign was already turned to closed. When she saw me, however, she came over and let us in.

"It's so good of you to keep checking on me, Janelle," she said, closing the blinds. "That makes a world of difference to my confidence."

I waved to Atticus as he emerged from the back room. "No more strange noises?"

"All the time. I'm getting used to it, though. Every so often I find a book lying on the floor. Usually the same one."

"*Romeo and Juliet*?" I asked, walking over to the bookshelf.

She shook her head. "*To Kill a Mockingbird*. One of my favorites, and I have many favorites. I reread them every year. They're my comfort food."

"A low-calorie solution." Smiling, I plucked the book from the shelf and then sat down with Bixby.

"I heard the bistro opening was a low-calorie evening, as well," Valerie said, kneeling to whisk dirt into her dustpan. "What a terrible shame."

Looking up from the book, I nodded. "The paramedics seemed to think Arnold Blatchford would recover. But Ethan Bogart is worried his restaurant won't fare as well."

"That's how I felt a few days ago about this place, but business gets better every day. If people are willing to overlook a murder for a cup of coffee, they'll do the same for Ethan's cooking. I hear he's very talented."

"That's what I told him. This is the kind of town where there are nearly as many tragedies as triumphs."

"That's what makes it exciting," she said, grinning now. "It's like living in a thriller novel."

I laughed as I flipped through the pages of the book.

Eventually Valerie got up and went into the back room, leaving me with the two dogs, one strangely quiet and the other more assertive.

Planting his beefy paw on the page, Bixby asked, "Are you avoiding going home?"

"I suppose so. Liberty is going to be riled up and I'd like to take a breather before dealing with her."

His paw was still on the book and I saw it had landed beside a heavily underlined word: "Watch."

"Huh," I told the dog, as I moved his paw and flipped further. "There are some random words underlined." I read them off silently. "Out. For. Angry." I kept flipping and found nothing more.

"Angry what?" Bixby said. "Is this a joke?"

"A prank, maybe." Starting at the beginning, I went page by page slowly and came up empty. Then, under the back dust jacket, I found one more word in strong lettering that looked familiar. "Gardeners."

"Watch out for angry gardeners?" Bixby asked.

"No question mark," I said. Indeed, there was a very pronounced period. That's how I knew for certain the message had come from Norris Strump, our very own Mr. Crossword, whose penmanship was confident and forceful.

"It's kind of vague," Bixby said.

I looked up as the door opened and clutched the dog tighter. "Not really. One angry gardener is dead and another just walked in."

CHAPTER TWENTY-EIGHT

"Hi, Sonia," I called. "The Beanstalk is closed. Valerie just let me in to borrow a book. I think I'm going to have trouble sleeping after what happened."

"Won't we all?" she said. "I'm still hungry after missing out on the free food, so I thought I'd see what's left here."

"I'm sure Valerie will be out in a minute." Getting up, I walked to the bookshelf. Before I could even replace the one I had, another dropped out. Collecting it, I went back to my seat, and started flipping. This time the underlined words fairly leapt off the page: "There's safety in numbers."

Pulling out my phone, I texted Ren to rally the troops, including the dogs.

Sonia tapped on the counter. "Where is she?"

"Just cleaning up, I think." I went to collect the next book Atticus tipped off the shelf.

"What is with those books?" she asked. "Are they falling off the shelf?"

I nodded. "There's a little vibration that shakes the bookcase. Like an earthquake only fun."

She gave me a strange look. "You should probably go home, Janelle."

Sitting down again, I flipped quickly. "Why?"

"Because the place is closed," she said. "Close your book."

The series of words underlined in this one didn't make sense to me, perhaps because I was increasingly nervous. I sent a silent message to Bixby to help me remember them.

"I haven't found just the right thing," I told Sonia as Atticus flipped another book off the shelf. "But the earthquake keeps on giving."

"There's no earthquake, but there is a curfew for people like you," she said.

I stared at her as I gathered Bixby under my arm and went to collect the book. "People like me? You mean the bookish type?"

She came a little closer. Her idea of dressing up for the restaurant opening included dirty boots and dried mud on her black pants. Her fingers were stained an odd orangey-brown shade. "I mean the nosy type. You're the wrong witch in every situation."

Logging in a few more words, I closed the book. "I'm becoming a connoisseur of fine words, Sonia, and I don't like that one. Never have, never will."

"I don't have time to dispute labels with you. I'm meeting some friends."

There was no point sitting down as Atticus had already flipped his next offering. "Don't let me hold you back."

She rolled her eyes. "I'm meeting friends *here*. So, be on your way. While you still can."

Flipping through the book, I collected three more words for my mental records. They were swimming in my head now, making no more sense than spells read backward. "That sounds vaguely threatening, Sonia, and I can't imagine you mean it that way."

Stomping toward me, she said. "Imagine I mean it that way. It will save time."

I replaced the book and bent to collect the next one that tumbled out. "Look at that mud from your shoes, Sonia. Valerie just swept."

The bell rang over the door while I was still bent over. "I thought the place was closed."

I knew the voice, although I'd only heard it while plucking memories from Mike and Ethan.

Straightening, I dug up a fake smile. "You must be Bucky Mulhairn. Brianna said so much about you that I'd know you anywhere." Brianna herself eased into the café behind him. "You'll be a comfort to her during these difficult times."

Brianna caught my eye and her expression was utterly miserable. "You and Mr. Bixby should go, Janelle," she said.

"Exactly," Sonia said. "And take the new owner with you."

"Sonia, it's her establishment," I said. "And we're all here after hours. We can't ask her to go."

I glanced at Atticus and told him to do what he could to chase Valerie out the back door. With his ghostly limitations, it wouldn't be easy, but all the dogs who wanted to cross back were smart cookies.

He knocked one last book out and then retreated to do as I asked.

"What's with those books?" Bucky said, as I replaced the ones I was still holding.

"I'm just here to borrow something to put me to sleep but they're a lively bunch," I said, laughing. "Are you a reader, Brianna?"

She shook her head. "Not really. I was always busy helping my grandmother in the garden."

"Wonderful. Did you inherit her green thumb?"

"I think so, yes." Brianna managed a smile. "She said I have a way with plants."

Scanning the last book quickly, I put it back. "Then it will make her proud to know you're taking over her greenhouse. From what I can tell, there's a pent-up demand for product."

"Bree doesn't have a head for business," Bucky said. "This is about more than playing with plants, so we're planning to sell."

Pressing the record button on my phone, I walked over to Brianna. She was being coerced into doing something she didn't want to do and I was here to support the underdog.

Mr. Bixby grumbled silently. "Must you? Always?"

I kept my focus on Bucky and Brianna. Touching the young woman's arm, my fingers started glowing. I hoped no one else noticed, but Brianna certainly felt it. She straightened and something lit her up inside.

"Do you want to run your grandmother's business, Brianna?" I asked.

She nodded. "That's what Grandma wanted. But Bucky wants to sell it to Sonia."

Sonia's eyes were fixed on me. "And I very much want to buy it. So we'll all be happy."

I shook my head. "Wait, did I miss something? The property belongs to Trina and Brianna. So they get to decide, right?"

"Grandma left the greenhouse to me," Brianna said. "And the house to my mom."

"Okay then. We know Maisie wanted you to have it and we know you want to keep it. I really am missing something."

"You're missing the part where you leave before you get hurt," Bucky said. "Stop putting ideas in my wife's head."

"Did the wedding happen today?" I asked. "Because it was still a dream yesterday."

"It's going to happen," Bucky said. "Just as soon as this transaction clears. How else could we pay for a wedding?"

"Weddings don't need to cost much at all," I said. "Wouldn't it be fun to have a ceremony in your very own garden, Brianna?"

"I suppose," she said. "Maybe in the summer."

The spark in her eyes dulled and I poured more energy into her arm.

"I thought you wanted to get married right away." Bucky's voice was too loud for the small café. "What's happened?"

Brianna still couldn't meet his eyes but she muttered, "I lost my grandmother. It changed everything."

Sonia's muddy boots turned. "And I'm giving you the opportunity of a lifetime. You'll never need to worry about money again after the sale is done."

"I don't worry about money now," Brianna said. "All I want to do is grow things, and now I can."

"There you have it," I said. "Brianna doesn't want to sell. Meeting adjourned."

Mr. Bixby laughed. "You don't expect it to end that easily, do you?"

I gave him a little squeeze, and backed away whispering, "It's just beginning, I fear."

CHAPTER TWENTY-NINE

The big question in my mind was who would be the first to lunge... Sonia or Bucky?

Unfortunately, the question made me so nervous I hiccupped, and sunflowers popped right out of the floor around Brianna's feet.

She didn't see them arrive because she was too busy trying to hold Bucky back. He dragged her over them, crushing the bright blooms, and then she looked down. Despite the circumstances, seeing the flowers made her smile. One bounced back up and started growing, which seemed to give her courage.

"Leave Janelle alone," she said, through clenched teeth. "She was just in the wrong place at the wrong time."

"Happens too much with Janelle," Sonia said. "There's only one way to make sure she doesn't end up that way again."

"Gillseed?" I asked. "I hear it's an efficient way to deal with inconveniences."

"Gillseed is one of the most toxic plants on the planet," Brianna said. "Even Grandma refused to grow it. She was always worried I'd get into it by mistake."

"Sonia took the risk," I said. "And I believe the police will find that's how Maisie died."

Brianna turned on Sonia. "You poisoned my grandma?"

The older woman shook her head. "I merely provided the means to an end. Likely a very uncomfortable end, I'm sorry to say, sweetpea. Maisie probably fought like a champ. I bet they found teaglove under her nails."

"An antidote," I said. "You nailed Oscar with gillseed too, didn't you?"

Sonia smirked. "He may have gotten a little hit when he tried to break into my greenhouse. Not quite enough, it seems."

Brianna still looked confused. "If you didn't poison my grandmother, Sonia... who did?"

Mr. Bixby swept his nose in the direction of Brianna's hulking fiancé and her eyes bulged. "Bucky? You killed my grandmother?"

"Of course not, Bree. I just did what Sonia asked and sprinkled some powder around." He turned to Sonia. "You said it was fertilizer. To maximize growth for the most valuable plants."

Sonia's barky laugh resembled a seal's. "Nice try, you fool."

"Let me get my facts straight," I said. "Bucky disabled security and broke into the greenhouse during the bridal shower to leave a toxic bomb for Maisie?"

"It was Sonia's idea," he said. "I just went along with it."

"Shut up, Bucky," Sonia said. "We have a deal and you'll keep your end of the bargain."

"He doesn't have that capacity," I said. "Because he doesn't own the property and now that Bree knows he colluded with you to kill Maisie... I expect he never will."

Bending, Brianna picked up a trampled sunflower. "That sounds about right. I'm marrying the greenhouse instead." Staring at Bucky's fingers on her arm, she said, "Let go of me."

"No, honey, I won't. We've made commitments we need to keep."

"*You* made commitments you can't keep." She jerked her arm

away. "If you kill me, you won't get my land, because we're not married."

"No one's planning on killing you, sweetpea," Sonia said. "You've always been a nice girl. A little dumb, but nice." She motioned to Bucky. "We'll just make her dumber. Easily enough done with the spoils of two greenhouses."

"Are you kidding me?" I said. "You can't sedate Brianna into complying with this."

"Just stay out of it, Janelle," Sonia said. "I'll get to you in time. First, we need a quick spell to settle Brianna down. Got herself all worked up for nothing."

She muttered an incantation and I watched with horror as the light dimmed in Brianna's eyes. Weaving unsteadily, Bree followed Bucky to a table and sat down.

"You just stay there, honey," he said. "It'll all be fine now. Sonia and I are going to deal with the mouthy witch."

"Which mouthy witch?" The voice rang out from the door. "You've got options." Cousin Liberty crunched toward us over sunflowers, clucking in disgust. "Oh, Janny, really?"

"I've got this, Cousin Liberty," I said, motioning for Sinda and Renata to stay near the door. Bijou was at Ren's side but Harold was conspicuously absent and likely to crop up just when we needed a good wind. "If you could just keep Ren and Sinda safe."

"They're fine and you'll be fine. I've always found Sonia supremely irritating, so I'll take her down first. The lunkhead hasn't a glimmer of magic so he'll be no fun at all."

The lunkhead might not be magical but he was fast on his feet for a big man. He yanked Brianna off the chair and held her in front of him like a floppy human shield. Then he pulled a knife from his pocket and held it to his fiancée's throat.

"Former fiancée," Mr. Bixby corrected. "What now?"

I expected Liberty to throw a curse, but Brianna suddenly turned from ragdoll to wildcat and elbowed Bucky in the gut. While he was reeling, she turned and kneed him even harder. He fell to his knees, groaning.

That's when Harold darted out from behind a table and created a wind barrier that included Sonia, too.

Sonia gaped at Brianna. "How did you—?"

"Rangleroot. Grandma always said, 'when in doubt, dose.'" Brianna tried to get around Harold to take on Sonia. "She also sent me for training in martial arts."

"Maisie was a smart woman," Liberty said. "Volatile but clever."

"I'm thinking you inherited more than her green thumb, Brianna," I said.

Unfortunately, martial arts wouldn't be enough to take down Sonia, who was likely packing gillseed somewhere right now. She was a botanical bomb waiting to go off.

Harold must have agreed because he pressed Sonia back, gently but persistently.

Sonia's face contorted and fear made me suck in a breath.

"Hold that hiccup, Janelle," Bixby said. "And step back."

Liberty charged at Sonia and the two women screeched unintelligibly at each other. If they were casting spells, they seemed to cancel each other out.

Meanwhile, I took Mike Spenser's advice and pulled in a breath, counting to six and releasing for eight. One more repetition and the compulsion to hiccup eased.

"Well done," Bixby said. "You've got this."

"I do?" My mind spun trying to figure out what he thought I had. "Ah. Yes. I do know."

I turned to the bookshelf and found Atticus poised to pounce. Bucky was crawling on his hands and knees toward Brianna, ready for one more go. Taking another deep breath, I bellowed, "Atticus. Come!"

There was that moment again where time seemed to slow and I watched the big white dog leap. Would he land where he belonged?

If where he belonged was bloodying Bucky, then he was definitely in the right place. I left him to it and turned back to Sonia.

Running my fingers along the bookshelf, I pulled the underlined words I needed from the classics and let them spill out of my lips.

Sonia stopped screaming. Her fingers clutched her throat and she collapsed.

"Finish the job," Bixby said. "I hate it when they bounce back after the big bang. Like in a B movie."

I bent over Sonia and sent a stunning shock of energy into her shoulder.

"For goodness' sake, Janelle," Liberty said. "Just kill the witch."

"I will not." Instead, I shooed Atticus away and stunned Bucky, too. The big dog loped over to Brianna. Her legs gave out and she welcomed him into her lap.

"Can I have him?" she asked.

"He's all yours," I said. "He chose you."

Liberty leaned over Sonia. "I'll do what you can't, Janelle."

Someone appeared in the doorway to the back room. "Did I come at a bad time?"

CHAPTER THIRTY

There was never a good time for Oscar Knight to arrive, in my opinion. In this case, we barely had the situation contained and he was another threat to handle.

"Or is he?" Mr. Bixby asked, from inside my head. "Where are the snakes? We didn't sense him coming."

I figured that was because of the adrenaline coursing through my veins, but after taking a deeper look, all I found in my mind were a few snakes coiled in the sun. Taking a little nap, as it were. They weren't gone but they weren't inclined to strike, either.

"Oscar, what did you do to Valerie?" I asked.

He came toward me, dusting flecks from his cashmere coat. "I took her to safety. She's my tenant and when I saw trouble on the security feed, I came right over." Glancing around, he said, "Care to explain what you're all doing on my premises?"

I shifted Mr. Bixby to cradle him with both arms. There would never be a time I didn't want my dog's protection against Oscar Knight.

"If I may, Oscar—" Liberty began.

He cut her off with a slash of one hand. "I was asking Janelle. I'm more likely to get a straight answer out of her."

"I'll tell you the truth," I said. "We've just apprehended Maisie Gledhill's killers. Brianna's fiancé joined forces with Sonia to poison Maisie." I shot Renata a questioning look and then added, "The police are on their way."

"My security officer is in the kitchen. I'll have him neutralize this room before that happens." Oscar pointed to the door. "All of you, *out*. Except Brianna."

I stared at him. "I won't leave, Oscar. This needs to be resolved officially so that Brianna can go on with her life. She inherited Maisie's greenhouse and will be starting it up again."

He stared down at Brianna, still sitting with Atticus in her lap. "That dog looks familiar. English setter?"

"I don't know," she said. "I just adopted him."

A circle of white appeared around Atticus's eyes and he growled at Oscar.

"Never liked that breed," Oscar said, backing up. "Young lady, I'd like to make you a very handsome offer on your property. I'm sure you've had others and I'll triple the highest. No questions asked."

She stared up at him over the dog's speckled ears. "Thank you, but it's not for sale. Grandma wanted me to run it and that's what I'll do."

"Brianna has Maisie's green thumb," I told Oscar. "The greenhouse will be in good hands."

He turned to me and his gray eyes glimmered with silver. The snakes in the sunshine woke up. "I didn't ask for your opinion on my business ventures, Janelle. Stick to selling pretty baubles at your little store."

"Oscar, that's no way to speak to someone who reversed your gillseed poisoning," I said. "I sent some teaglove home with Tavi, and look at you now. All threatening again."

"Teaglove she probably took from me," Liberty said, coming up beside me. "Luckily she left enough for Arnold Blatchford. You gentlemen are indebted to the Brighton women tonight."

Oscar's mouth worked as he tried to figure out his next move. "I don't like debts," he said at last. "I'd rather clear the slate by letting you all walk out alive."

Liberty laughed. "You and your cronies may have taken me down once but you're hardly a match for two of us.

"Four of us," Sinda called. "And more."

Brianna pushed herself off the floor. "Thank you, everyone, but I can speak for myself. Finally. Turns out my fiancé was dosing me with something to make me... I don't know... docile? Placid?"

"Cooperative," I said. "And you countered it."

She nodded. "After meeting you, I suddenly realized my spark was gone. I took something to clear the fog and then used our reserved cache of rangleroot. Mr. Knight, with all due respect, I don't intend to be manipulated again."

"I'm offering you a huge sum—enough to live a life of luxury anywhere in the world."

She shrugged. "This is where we belong. Atticus and me. Running our greenhouse and making sure people get the plants they need. I'll be doing things differently from now on. You'll get your rangleroot at more reasonable prices. My grandmother was a shrewd businesswoman and she kept supply limited. I plan to expand access, and you're our biggest client, Mr. Knight."

"Why do you need all that rangleroot, Oscar?" Liberty asked.

"None of your business." His eyes fell to the dog in Brianna's lap. "You're calling this thing Atticus?"

"That's his name. He came that way." She smiled as she ran a hand over his back and his feathery tail came up. "We're a team now."

Oscar shook his head and then frowned as the sound of sirens reached us. "I'm missing a few pieces of a puzzle and I intend to find them."

"How about you turn your focus to something useful?" Liberty said. "When I escaped your prison, I made a decision to make a difference. And the mayor's asked me to join an advisory committee to re-envision this town. Why don't you throw your hat into the ring?"

He ran a hand over his always-perfect hair. "I declined. I'm not a team player."

"That's not true," Liberty said. "You just team up with the wrong people. I did that, too, long ago but one thing you did for me was give me time to think. And I want to go a different way."

That surprised me as much as it seemed to surprise Oscar. His nostrils flared as if sniffing for deception, and then his shoulders squared.

Mr. Bixby chuckled. "He's not going to let Liberty squirm into the mayor's good graces without him."

"A genius move by Mayor Longmuir," I replied. "Get the combustibles contained on one committee."

The squad cars pulled up out front. I pointed to Oscar and then Liberty. "Let me handle this. It's my mess."

"It's your win," Liberty said. "I'm proud of you." She glared at her new ally. "Don't take this away from her, Oscar."

He walked over and sat down in my usual chair. "Just here to watch the show play out."

While the paramedics examined Sonia and Bucky, Drew came over. "Wait, don't tell me, Janelle. They'll be too addled to make a bit of sense when they wake up."

"*If* they wake up," Liberty said. "They don't really deserve to see daylight."

"Liberty." I pinched her arm. "Chief Gillock doesn't understand your sense of humor."

"She doesn't have a sense of humor," Oscar said. "Not to my recollection."

Drew pointed at Liberty and then Oscar. "When I need to hear from you, I'll ask."

Liberty checked her reflection in the window and then smoothed her gray coronet. "That's shortsighted of you, young man. You could learn a lot about this town from me. And even, perhaps, Oscar Knight."

Oscar acknowledged her with a slight nod. "Although there are still things I don't know. Like why this dog looks so similar to the one my wife loved decades ago. And has the same name."

"A coincidence," I said. "Atticus is a popular name among bookish dog lovers like Tavi."

He rolled his eyes. "And English setters are hip again?"

"Were they ever?" Liberty asked. "Pretty but useless."

I pinched her harder. "He's far from that. And I don't think the chief is interested in dogs right now. He'd like to know about how Sonia and Bucky killed Maisie."

"I would, indeed," Drew said. "Is there any chance at all of getting a straight answer?"

"No," Liberty and Oscar said at once, and both looked chagrined as their voices overlapped.

"Yes." The affirmative answer came not from me, but from Brianna. "I want to tell you everything that happened, starting with how my fiancé played me." Tears filled her eyes and rolled down her cheeks. "And Sonia was the mastermind with the poison. They killed my grandmother to take what's rightfully mine."

He glanced at me and I pulled out my phone. "It's all here, Chief. Along with some strange things you may not want to hear."

"Janelle," Liberty said, reaching for the phone. "Give me that."

Oscar was out of his chair in a flash, trying to grab for it, too.

"Stand down, Mr. Knight," Drew said, sliding my phone into his pocket. "And you, Miss Brighton the senior."

Her faced flushed. "Do not call me that."

"Just to distinguish from Miss Brighton the junior," he said.

"Good one, Red." Bixby chuckled. "But she'll make you regret it. Expect boils in uncomfortable places. Or perhaps a rack of antlers for Christmas."

Liberty crossed her arms. "I don't like you, young man. You're over—"

"Overreaching. I know." Drew shrugged. "That's what a visiting police chief needs to do to keep his head above water in a town like this."

"Go ahead," Oscar said. "But many drown in Wyldwood's wonderful springs."

Drew turned his dark eyes on the older man. "Mr. Knight, *you're* overreaching. I suggest you go home to your wife. One of my officers found her wandering and took her home."

I didn't think Oscar was capable of scrambling, but after a brief tussle with some chairs, he bolted into the night.

Mr. Bixby and the other dogs all laughed, and Atticus said, "Good riddance."

"The rest of you can sit down," Drew said. "We have some talking to do."

Ren came forward. "Would it be okay if I put on some coffee? I know my way around this place."

Drew nodded and went to check out the back room.

I took the opportunity to put the books in order before joining the others at the table Oscar had vacated.

"How did you know that spell?" Liberty whispered. "It's most certainly not in my primer for novices."

I ran my hand over the English setter's sleek head. "I had some help."

At that moment, a man appeared outside the door. I expected to see Oscar's henchman, but it was Mr. Crossword, Norris Strump. I gestured to his usual seat but he shook his head. Then he touched his fedora and bowed slightly. I pressed my fingers to my lips and pretended to throw a kiss.

"What's going on?" Liberty said. "Are you lightheaded? At risk of floral eruptions?"

I laughed. "Nope. Just building my new community, one wonderful person at a time."

Brianna reached out to take my hand and squeezed it with murmured thanks.

"Oh, stop," Liberty said. "Too much sentiment makes me queasy."

"Me too," Mr. Bixby said. "As much as I hate to agree with Liberty."

"Remember, this is Wyldwood," Liberty added. "There's another vile varmint around every corner."

I smiled at Brianna. "Do you have something for that?"

"Every poison you could ever imagine. And a few you couldn't."

"Now that's a sentiment I can get behind," Liberty said, settling back and crossing her arms. "Do tell us more."

Brianna scratched Atticus' speckled ears. "Nope. My dog only wants me to talk antidotes."

CHAPTER THIRTY-ONE

Two days later, after the police tape was down, Renata and I showed up bright and early at the Beanstalk Café. Norris Strump had beaten us there, as usual, and ignored me completely when I passed.

"Hey, Mr. Crossword," Bixby said, leaning out of my arms to try to nip the man's fedora. "We're done with your hattitude."

Norris jerked his head aside and continued etching his answers into the newspaper with a ballpoint pen.

"Discourteous," I said. "That's five down."

The pen lifted and hovered. "I hate it when you do that," he said.

It was the first time he'd spoken to me directly. "I know. That's why I do it. You gave me words when I needed them and I'm happy to toss a few your way."

"Please. Do me the courtesy of holding them back." He pushed the paper aside. "Now you've ruined the whole thing."

"Oh Norris, don't be cranky," I said. "This time I was messing with you. Five down only takes six letters. Starting with —"

"Go have your coffee," he said. "Because you're going to need it shortly."

"Please. Do me the courtesy of letting me be surprised by life."

Grinning, I walked on to my favorite table and set Mr. Bixby and my purse on the bench.

"Life is better with fewer surprises," Norris said. "Although there was a sunflower blooming under my table this morning. That was nice."

Nice for him, but somewhat disheartening for me. I thought I had nipped that problem in the bud. My breathing exercises were doing wonders for both my diaphragm and my peace of mind. Brianna had come by to talk to the police and sprinkled a magical flower control agent around the café. A floricide, she called it.

"I hope it only kills flowers," Mr. Bixby said. "This place can't take another hit to its reputation."

"It'll be fine." I took off my coat and draped it over my purse. "In Wyldwood notoriety can work for you, too. I'm counting on it to help with our stores, as well as Ethan's bistro."

"Much depends on Oscar," Bixby said.

"So much. Too much."

I went back to the counter to collect my coffee. Valerie Fairchild was smiling rather vacantly, likely an unwitting recipient of Oscar's memory spell. When she visited Whimsy yesterday, Ren had offered to step in and help Val get back on her feet at the Beanstalk. Now my best friend was serving customers while Valerie wandered around with a broom and dustpan. Somehow she had missed the sunflower under Norris' table.

Bijou left Ren to join Bixby and me. "You're a hero, my girl," I told her. "Sniffing out that poison not only saved Arnold and us, but probably many others. Brianna said a pinch can take down a crowd, and Sonia was willing to clear cut the party to get the garden she wanted."

"I'm the one who identified the toxin," Bixby said. "Why does the poodle get the glory? I'm also the one who slipped you the answers in the ultimate test."

"You did, too," I said. "I don't know where I'd be without you, Bixby. Definitely not sitting here enjoying a coffee on a beautiful morning. I'm lucky to have such an awesome canine team."

"Sip faster," Bixby said. "Mr. Crossword was right about things taking a turn."

I felt Oscar Knight before I saw him, but the snakes were coiled today as he held the door open for Octavia, and then followed her in. The silk scarf, sunglasses and trench coat were gone. Her highlighted blonde hair gleamed and she looked like a younger version of the woman who'd come into my store weeks ago. On the way to the table, she stooped and planted a loud smooch on Norris' cheek.

"Ten down. Affection," she said.

"Twelve across. Annoying," he replied, batting her away.

The exchange made me wonder if the project of planting clues in books had been a joint effort.

"We hoped to find you here," Tavi said, letting her coat fall off her shoulders in full confidence that her husband would catch it.

He did just that. "Tavi hoped to find you here. I can always do without seeing you. Except on the Christmas planning committee."

"Speaking of the holidays, I'd love to have you and your crew for Thanksgiving dinner," she said, sitting down. "You, too, Norris. Twenty across. Turkey."

"Thirty down. Vegan," he called back. "I've got plans. I'm not one of your strays, Tavi."

"Speaking of strays." Tavi rested her elbows on the table and fixated on me. "Oscar told me about Atticus, the English setter you apparently placed with Brianna."

"That dog always hated me," Oscar said, still standing. "How did he end up here?"

I smiled up at him. "I have no idea, Oscar. Truly."

Now he perched on a chair. "You're saying a rather uncommon dog who looks and acts like my wife's dearly departed Atticus just turned up here at the Beanstalk?"

"That's exactly what happened," I said, shrugging. "I can't explain it. He took a shine to Brianna and she needs him."

"She needs more help than a goofy English setter can give her," Oscar said. "She's in way over her head with that operation."

"Don't be so sure of that. She has a botany degree and Maisie's been training her since childhood. And what she *didn't* teach her in business will serve us well."

He turned his chair slightly in the direction of Norris and when the old man stared, switched to the other direction. "Whatever."

"Oscar, I heard you got a good supply of rangleroot from Brianna's smaller greenhouse, and you didn't need to break into Liberty's house to get it. I'd call that a win."

His wife stared at his profile. "Why do you need so much rangleroot that you'd consider stealing from Liberty?"

"It's a protective root, darling," he said. "We need plenty in stock for my line of work."

"Only you go through it like crazy," I said. "No bigger consumer, apparently."

He turned back so abruptly the chair nearly tipped. "She shouldn't be talking about her customers' purchasing habits. It's unprofessional."

"I have other ways of collecting information. And I'm super curious about why you need so much of it."

Octavia tipped her head. "Me too, Oscar. Please enlighten us."

"We'll talk about it at home," he said. "Have you forgotten our feud with the Brightons?"

"I've forgotten a lot of things," she said. "But not that. And Liberty will make sure I never do."

I reached into my purse and pulled out Octavia's rings. Oscar reached for them but she swatted his hand away.

"Just explain, Oscar," I said. "Tavi deserves to know before she decides whether or not to put these back on."

"Deserves to know what?" she said. "Nothing can be worse than leaving Liberty's dog to die. That's why these rings came off."

He slumped in his seat. "You only heard one side of the story. As a gentleman, I defer to Liberty to explain the rest."

"Start with the rangleroot," I said. "I'm worried about Philomena."

"Our dog? Why?" he asked. "She's fine."

"She's not fine," Octavia said. "I took her to the vet yesterday with a rash."

I sighed. "Unless I'm much mistaken, she's getting double dosed with rangleroot. There's no standard treatment information for canines."

"You're treating Philomena?" Tavi asked her husband.

"Of course. You love your dog and I want her to be safe. I worried Liberty would come after her."

"She wouldn't," I said. "But you two should be talking about these things, for the good of the dog. And for the good of Octavia, too."

Turning back to me, her lips pressed into a thin line. "What are you saying, Janelle?"

I gestured to Oscar. "Ask your husband where the rest of the rangleroot goes."

She stared at him and after a heavy sigh, he answered. "Into your tea every morning, Tavi. Plus into a protein supplement I send regularly to Jared. I'm trying to keep my family safe, that's all."

After a few minutes that felt like ages to me and probably longer to Oscar, she said, "How long? How long have you been drugging me? You've been serving me tea for over thirty years."

He nodded. "At your mother's request. She worried about you."

Octavia sank back in her chair. "My mother? I don't understand any of this."

I reached out and touched her arm, half expecting her to pull away. Instead, she let whatever energy I had sink into her, and finally added, "Why?"

Oscar was staring silently at his hands so I explained. "He's protecting you because your mother underestimated your magical ability to do that for yourself."

Her chin lifted slightly. "How do you underestimate nothing?"

I squeezed her arm harder and laughed. "It's only nothing because you've been told that all your life. Trust me, there's something."

Oscar flicked my fingers off Tavi's arm. "Don't tell her that. Don't you dare mislead my wife. She could be hurt."

"Your keeping secrets from her is hurting her more. And I'm willing to bet a good portion of the trouble you get into is about trying to keep her safe, when she might very well be able to do that herself. Especially if you stopped stirring things up."

"You don't know what you're talking about," he said, starting to rise.

"I know you were pretty desperate to get your hands on Maisie's land, in competition with Arnold and Sonia."

"Don't forget Liberty," he spat back. "She was bidding on the land, too. And it's not all about rangleroot."

"Everyone had different motivations. For you, it's mainly about protecting those you love. Could be worse."

"Tavi, let's go."

His wife slid the rings toward him. "You can keep these until I've heard everything Janelle has to say. I've been feeling fresher since the tea shortage began and have decided to keep it that way."

Oscar sat back down. Hard. "Fresher?"

"Sharper. Happier. I don't really know how to explain it."

I touched her arm again. "You feel like yourself. And now, with Oscar's help, you can explore the extent of your abilities. Drug-free."

Oscar buried his face in his hands. "I've never..."

He didn't want to tell his wife that he'd felt no magic in her.

"I have," I insisted. "She has magic but she can't access it if she's bogged down by your fears and spells. Walk the path with her and help. That's what my family is doing with me."

She grabbed my hand. "Just one more question. If my mother was wrong about me... was everyone wrong about Jared?"

Mr. Bixby piped up in my head. "Now, that's a very good question. Someone may have just unleashed a genie from a bottle."

Across the café, Norris muttered, "Thirty-two down. Aladdin."

CHAPTER THIRTY-TWO

The bell over the door gave its merriest jingle as Liberty walked into Whimsy two days later. The clock had yet to hit seven a.m., but she was wearing a green jacket over a green dress that shimmered. Her hair was perfect, her makeup on point and her heels enviable. She wouldn't have looked out of place for a Broadway premiere but it was a little much for the impromptu opening of Flour Girl Bakery. Ren had decided to throw the doors open early to supply the Beanstalk Café as well.

"Why are you staring?" Liberty asked. "And why on earth did you dress down for the biggest day in your best friend's life?"

I was wearing a nice dress, nicer coat, my nicest heels... and a snazzy dachshund. "I look fine. My best friend has to rock a hairnet, so I'm not going to overdo it. All eyes should be on the star of the hour."

"Eyes are on the Brightons all the time," she said, coming to the counter with Harold. "Oscar Knight may be vanquished but someone will fill the vacuum and we need to look our best when the time comes."

"I don't think we can definitely say Oscar is vanquished." I buttoned my coat for the short walk next door. "He's subsided, that's all. Recalibrating."

"Piffle." She pulled out a compact. "I got that word from your dog, you know."

"I can hear you," Bixby said, aloud. "Feel free to give me credit directly when you steal my material."

She looked at him over the hand mirror. "Harold is such a wonderful support without a shred of vanity."

"He's a working breed," I said. "Each of my dogs is special in a different way."

Now she looked over the mirror at me. "*My* dog. Make no mistake."

"Hers, too," Harold said, simply.

Mr. Bixby actually waited a beat in case Harold wanted to say more. But he hated a vacuum, too. "Our family matriarch has enough vanity for all of us."

She snapped the compact shut and dropped it in her purse. "Just the right amount to keep up appearances in this town." She clicked to the door. "I've joined the Christmas planning committee, by the way. Ruthann insisted. Vanity would tell me she values my insights, but I know full well she just wants to keep an eye on all of us."

"I think you're right about that. Apparently Arnold Blatchford got an invitation, too. This committee is like school detention."

Reaching up, Liberty gave the bell a tickle and it gurgled with glee. "I'll have to take your word for it, since I was kicked out of school in third grade. Or was it second? Either way, I have no knowledge of formal education systems."

I moved Bixby to my hip and followed her to the door. "You're no slouch in the brains department, Liberty. Who's your pick for the next Wyldwood bad boy?"

"My money's on—"

"Don't say Jared Knight. I couldn't bear it. He chased me out of this town and made me a nomad."

She used one manicured index finger to lift my chin. "No one did that but you, my dear. That said, if I hadn't gotten myself into trouble with his father, I'd have kicked that young oaf to the curb. I do regret not being there for you. I've turned over a new leaf."

"You sure have," Bixby said, nudging her finger away from me. "From gone to constant presence."

"Quiet, fool," she said. "I had to move back into the manor because Janelle was so upset over the purloined dining room set."

I laughed, knowing Liberty had her own reasons that didn't include my feelings about furniture. "There's plenty of room for you at the manor and I'm glad you brought a table to serve Thanksgiving dinner on tomorrow. As our matriarch."

"I expect things will go better if Renata's at the helm," she said, leading me out. "We came so close to poisoning already without adding my cooking to it."

She stood back to let me open the door to Flour Girl, so that she could make an entrance. I figured it would be for an audience of one, but others had beaten us into the bakery. Valerie was behind the counter helping Ren, and the two worked like a well-oiled machine to serve a small lineup that included Sinda, Brianna, Norris Strump, and the two police chiefs. Ethan Bogart was managing the coffee station.

"How nice to have a police presence," Liberty said. "Your croissants are safe, Renata."

"Not safe from consumption, I hope," Ren said. "I'd like every last one to be gone by noon."

Chief Dredger blew plenty of crumbs around, which made Atticus happy. Of all the dogs I'd brought back, he was the hungriest.

"And the most useless," Bixby said, not bothering to use his inside voice. "I think you made a mistake with that one."

Sinda shook her finger at him. The English setter had been among her jewels and was now dangling from a chain around Brianna's neck as she placed her order.

"Young lady," Liberty said, tapping Brianna's shoulder. "I'd like to hire you as a consultant as I build my own greenhouse."

Brianna inspected her Danish before answering. "I'm not consulting. I don't want to take orders from anyone anymore. But if I can share cuttings without damaging my own plants, I'm happy to do it. For Janelle, and also to keep the peace in town."

"We appreciate that," Drew said. "Wyldwood is overdue for some peace."

He stayed behind while Chief Dredger left to carry a bag to Officer Barrow, who was standing on the street, nearly out of view. With the quality of the baked goods, it wouldn't be long before Jimmy got over himself and placed his order directly. Renata was about to get busier than she'd ever been before.

I accepted the pastries she gave me and moved over to the window seat, hoping to have a moment alone with Drew.

"You're never alone with a pedigreed dachshund in your head and your arms," Bixby reminded me. "Both hands, please. I feel vulnerable today."

"Just simmer down," I whispered. "You're getting the chatline pinch to be sure of it."

"Wait, wait. You'll want to hear this: I see a sunflower sprouting out of the window seat."

I spun quickly, hoping Bixby was pranking me, but sure enough a small but rather sturdy specimen was poking through floral fabric. "I didn't hiccup. Not even close."

"Maybe not physically, but emotionally," he said. "Deep breathing may not be enough to save your pride."

There was a skirmish of fluff as Harold blew Bijou over. "Leave Witchy alone, wiener boy," she said, hopping onto the window seat.

The poodle grabbed the stem of the flower in her jaws and snapped it off.

I clutched my chest and gasped. "I felt that."

"Oh, great," Bixby said. "Now she's getting all emotional over broken flowers."

A voice behind me said, "What's going on?"

Bijou jumped off the window seat and then hopped around in a full circle with the sunflower in her jaws. When she was done, she dropped it at Drew's feet.

Smiling, the chief bent to pick it up and presented it to me.

"Sweet, but confusing," Bixby said, inside my head. "You spontaneously grew the flower he's giving you. Isn't life complicated?"

I decided to let it be simple for a change and thanked Drew. Then I set Bixby on the window seat. Bijou, Harold and Atticus all joined him, and they sat there with paws hanging over the edge. The three dogs kept moving to cover sunflower sprouts, whereas Bixby did the opposite and even poked his long nose at a boisterous shoot, hoping Drew would notice.

"I heard Ethan's bistro has been cleared to open again," I said. "He deserves a better start."

"He does and it couldn't have been much worse," Drew said. After a moment, he self-corrected. "Scratch that. No one died."

"And no one died at the Beanstalk this time, so it's all systems go," I said.

"Maybe. I hope so." He stared around. "I don't know. Something's still making me uneasy."

A little shiver ran through me and I nodded. "Me too, suddenly. It's like a cloud passed over the sun." I glanced out the window and pointed. "I think we have our answer."

He turned and we both stared at Officer Slick. Oscar's henchman was wearing his secret police uniform, with the small neon insignia.

"I thought we were done with him," I said, as much to Mr. Bixby as Drew. "Oscar has backed off me a bit."

"Oh?" Drew's auburn eyebrows rose. "As evidenced by what?"

"For starters, he found me a tenant for the vacant store. Another florist."

Mr. Bixby pawed at me to be lifted, and more specifically, inserted into the conversation. "You mean a spy."

Drew continued to stare out at Slick, before saying, "You mean a spy."

"Aha! I knew Big Red could hear me." Bixby immediately asked to be deposited on the window seat again, so he could prance around in glee. "Life is about to get so interesting. Bijou, grab me a boutonniere for my collar."

"Don't be stupid, little sausage. It was just a coincidence."

I tended to agree with Bijou. Drew otherwise showed no signs of hearing the canine element of the conversation.

"Coincidence," Harold agreed. "But there's more to the chief than meets the eye."

"Or sniffer," Bijou said. "Your guy has a secret, Witchy."

Mr. Bixby shoved her. "If Red has a secret, I'll be the first to notice and inform Janelle." The dachshund walked over and sniffed Drew's dangling fingertips. "Hmmm... You might be right."

"Maybe he's married," Atticus said. "With a bunch of redheaded kids."

Bixby tipped his head. "Could be. Happens all the time."

Bijou directed a sharp bark at each of them. "If he were married, Witchy would feel it. She's a psychic, remember."

"Would she, though?" Bixby asked. "This psychic has errati-cally shot up a dozen flowers today. She's not working at her peak."

The dog wasn't wrong and it didn't help that I was afraid to get too close to Drew at all now.

"Wise," Bixby said. "Or he could sprout one out his ear. Or nose. Can you imagine?" He paused. "I am imagining it right now."

There was a better than fair chance that might have happened had Octavia Knight not arrived and saved me from myself. She dashed over to Atticus, arms outstretched. The big dog backed away until he fell off the window seat and skulked over to Brianna. It's a good thing she was a tall girl, because the setter wedged himself between her knees.

"That's my dog," Octavia said, kneeling. "Well, one of them. Atticus, come here and say hi to mama."

"Tavi, stand up darling," Oscar said, pulling gently on her shoulder. "It's a doppelgänger. Your English setter passed years and years ago."

Atticus fanned the floor gently with his tail as he stared sadly at Octavia, but the fanning stopped when his eyes landed on Oscar. The whites showed again.

"See, it is our dog," Octavia said. "He was always scared of you."

"Darling, most dogs are scared of me," Oscar said. "That's why I love Philomena. She's the only one who sees I'm a sweetheart."

Mr. Bixby hacked dramatically and strutted closer to Oscar. "Not scared, dude."

Harold wasn't scared, either. He moved into a pounce position, in case he had to create a wind disturbance.

That would have spelled doom for all the pastries on open trays, so I stepped in. "Tavi, it sounds like this dog is very similar to your beloved Atticus, but you have the right dog in Philomena. I'm sure the similarity has brought up some old feelings, because you told me you wanted more for Atticus."

She nodded. "I did say that. Jared and Oscar didn't like him much and things were a little tense at home. The dog would act out sometimes."

"Chewed up the left shoe of every pair I owned," Oscar said. "And regularly pooped in my slippers."

We all laughed, even his wife. "I hope this dog has a good life."

Brianna smiled. "He does and he will. We're best friends already. I never felt safe before he came along."

Straightening, Tavi walked over and squeezed Brianna's arm. That's when I noticed the rings were back on her finger. "A dog definitely makes things easier."

"There are too many dogs in here," Oscar said. "I would never have allowed it when I owned the place. Someone might contact the health authorities."

"But someone won't," Liberty called from the coffee station, where Ethan was serving strong, hot brew. "Because someone would be stupid to raise trouble for good people and their therapy dogs. Wouldn't you agree, Tavi?"

"I absolutely would, Liberty," Octavia said. "I'm pursuing therapy certification for Philomena as well."

Renata came around the counter to join us with Sinda. "Welcome to Flour Girl, Mr. and Mrs. Knight. Please come and choose a treat. Some things are already selling out."

"I'm so thrilled for you, Ren," I said, as Sinda led the Knights away. "How does it feel?"

"Awesome." Her white teeth gleamed. "It's the best day ever. And tomorrow will be wonderful, too. I can't wait to cook Thanksgiving dinner. You're coming, Drew?"

He nodded. "Wouldn't miss it. Well, I'll miss half of it because I'm working overnight. But I'll be there." Reaching for my sleeve, he tugged gently. "Could I have a word with you? Alone?"

"Excuse me," Bixby roared up at him with ferocious yapping. "Earth to Big Red. I have a celestial contract with Janelle and there's no such thing as alone."

My heart started to race as I imagined the bad news he wanted to break to me privately.

"He's not married with kids," Bijou said. "I know what dads smell like."

I pressed my lips together but it didn't stop the hiccup. Behind the dogs on the bench, things were popping.

Ren started pushing me out of the bakery. "Go next door to Whimsy, where it's quiet."

My dachshund's hysteria on the window seat was going to drive her clients away. "Grab Bixby for me, will you?" I whispered.

She went to collect the dog and came back with Bixby under one arm and sunflowers under the other. In a moment of confusion, she handed the dog to Drew and the sunflowers to me.

We quickly switched and he stared at the flowers, over a foot long, with roots dangling. Since he couldn't think of anything else to do with them, he kept them as we walked the few feet to Whimsy's door. I unlocked it and stepped in with Bixby, who was still grumbling, and Drew followed.

After setting the dog on the counter, I took the flowers from Drew and shoved them into a vase, roots and all. It was a haphazard and somewhat ratty bouquet—not at all like the pretty bunch he'd given me when my store opened.

"Get him talking," Bixby said. "Or that vase is going to get mighty crowded."

Taking a couple of deep breaths, I smiled. "What did you want to tell me?"

He paced in front of the counter a few times and then reached out to take my hand. At first I worried about dirt on my fingers, but of course the flowers had burst from the seat cushion and were artificially clean.

After a second, I stopped worrying. The sunshine I always felt in Drew's presence intensified. Heat flooded through my hand and up my arm to my heart. Whatever he wanted to say, it wasn't horrible. There was no abandoned family down south.

"It's about the recording you shared," he said.

"The confession, yes."

"I know there was a lot going on that night. Do you remember the conversation?"

I shook my head. "Not all of it. I assume there were some surprises."

"Very much so. I wanted to preserve the confession, which fits with the evidence and history. But there was some reference to magic."

"Okay," Bixby said. "This is going to get awkward."

I ignored the dog and thought about what to say. There was a time for evasion and a time for coming clean. This felt like the latter. With so many suspicious deaths between us, I was done with sidestepping. Could the bond between us hold up to the truth?

"Bombs away," Bixby said. "Let the chips fall where they may."

"Magic," I said. "I'm not surprised. This town is full of magic, and not always the good kind."

His dark eyes were serious. "And you?"

I nodded. "Full of it. By birthright."

"The good kind?" he asked.

"I like to think so. I've helped you put away some terrible people. Criminals in every sense of the word. But I guess that will ultimately be for you to decide."

He held up our laced fingers. "I guess I already knew. Your hands tingle."

"My hands tingle?"

Mr. Bixby stuck his long nose between us. "Surely I mentioned that? But tingling is pretty normal to me."

"They do. Just like my mother's," Drew said.

Bixby chortled. "And Big Red presents another plot twist. Love it."

"Your mother?" I said. "How interesting. And was she a good person?"

"She liked to think so, but she died too young. Because of that magic."

"Drew, I'm sorry. I didn't know. Unfortunately, accidents do happen where there's magic."

"That's why I've been on the fence. I wasn't sure I could lose someone to magic again."

"I understand completely. It's not something I wanted. Came with the Brighton package."

His eyes dropped to my fingers, which he was squeezing tighter than ever. "Do you want to talk about it?"

"Not really," I said. "Not right now, anyway. Can you use the confession?"

He nodded. "I worked a little magic of my own."

Bixby chipped in. "For reals?"

"I mean I was able to redact the questionable bits," Drew said. "It's certainly not something I'm going to brag about but it put two deadbeats behind bars."

"Okay, good," I said. "So, what do we do now?"

"About the string of deadbeats... or the tingling?"

I pushed Mr. Bixby's snout out of the way. "Both, I guess."

"You could try to stay out of trouble," Drew said. "Would that be asking too much?"

I laughed. "Yeah. Not an option. Trouble finds me."

"I figured. And I'm glad to put trouble away for you. So, carry on."

He was pulling me closer and the sleek black snout managed to find a little room between us. Then the dog unleashed a deep bark that made us both jump.

"Someone is not on board with tingling of any sort," Drew said.

"Correct," Bixby said. "Score one point for Big Red."

I pulled Drew away from the counter. "That someone is not me. I'm definitely on board. Did you know your hands tingle, too? Your mom left something behind."

He stopped and his eyes widened. "Oh?"

"Way to ruin a moment, Janelle," Bixby called after me. "And here I thought I was going to have to do the heavy lifting."

I continued on, regardless. "It's what makes you so good at your job, Drew."

"Mostly training and experience, I would think."

"With a little extra, that's all. It's how you keep a clear head when the going gets murky."

His eyes shifted to the window and his lips pressed together. "A little extra. Okay. Well, you've given me something to think about."

He let go of my hand and a chill set in instantly. I backed up till I hit the counter and Bixby leaned against my upper arm. "Don't be sad. We're meant to be lone wolves."

"Let's talk more tomorrow night. At Thanksgiving," Drew said, pulling the door open. "There's more to be thankful about this year than ever before."

My heart lit up with gratitude. Lone wolf no more. "I agree."

"You're so right, buddy," Bixby called after him. "You got the girl, the magic and the dog all on one day. Don't wait to give thanks."

"Thanks," Drew said. As the door closed behind him, he added, "That dog is something else."

I turned and scooped the dog off the counter. "He sure is."

"You may hug me once," Bixby said. "It's a big day."

I hugged him many times and threw in a couple of kisses over his objections.

"Fine, whatever," he said, when I finally set him down. "I'm thankful for you, too. Don't let it go to your head."

Grabbing clippers off a shelf, I trimmed the roots and arranged the sunflowers nicely. The blooms had doubled in size and filled out.

"Enough already," Bixby said. "Go get the spell book and let's see what can be done about hiccups."

"You're on," I said. "Wake up Wyldwood, I'm spelling again."

Join Janelle and Mr. Bixby on their next great adventure in *Do You Haunt to Know a Secret?* A haunted library, a bossy new mentor and uncontrollable magical hiccups are just the beginning of the challenges facing this novice witch and her sassy canine sidekick as the Mystic Mutts Series continues. Don't miss the fun!

Want to hear what comes next for Janelle, Mr. Bixby and the Wyldwood gang? Join my Ellen Riggs newsletter at **ellenriggs.com/mystic-mutts-opt-in** to get the latest news. You'll also get to read plenty of free stories, including the prequels to my Bought-the-Farm and Dog Town mystery series for pet-lovers. Hope to see you there!

More Books by Ellen Riggs

Mystic Mutt Mysteries Paranormal Cozy

- I Want You to Haunt Me
- You Can't Always Get What You Haunt
- Any Way You Haunt It
- I Only Haunt to be with You
- All I Haunt Is You
- Do You Haunt to Know a Secret?
- All I Haunt for Christmas

Bought-the-Farm Cozy Mystery Series

- A Dog with Two Tales (*prequel*)
- Dogcatcher in the Rye
- Dark Side of the Moo
- A Streak of Bad Cluck
- Till the Cat Lady Sings
- Alpaca Lies
- Twas the Bite Before Christmas
- Swine and Punishment
- The Cat and the Riddle
- Don't Rock the Goat
- Swan with the Wind
- How to Get a Neigh with Murder
- Tweet Revenge
- For Love Or Bunny
- Between a Squawk and a Hard Place
- Double Dog Dare
- Deerly Departed
- Think Outside the FoxMouse of Ill Repute
- Bee All and End All
- Sheep with One Eye Open
- Roo the Day

Bought-the-Farm Mysteries - Boxed Sets

- Bought the Farm Mysteries - Books 1-3
- Bought the Farm Mysteries - Books 4-6
- Bought the Farm Mysteries - Books 7-9
- Bought the Farm Mysteries - Books 10-12
- Bought the Farm Mysteries - Books 13-15
- Bought the Farm Mysteries - Books 1-10

Books by Ellen Riggs and Sandy Rideout

Dog Town Series

- Ready or Not in Dog Town (The Beginning)
- Bitter and Sweet in Dog Town (Labor Day)
- A Match Made in Dog Town (Thanksgiving)
- Lost and Found in Dog Town (Christmas)
- Calm and Bright in Dog Town (Christmas)
- Tried and True in Dog Town (New Year's)
- Yours and Mine in Dog Town (Valentine's Day)
- Nine Lives in Dog Town (Easter)
- Great and Small in Dog Town (Memorial Day)
- Bold and Blue in Dog Town (Independence Day)
- Better or Worse in Dog Town (Labor Day)

Dog Town Boxed Sets

- Mischief in Dog Town - Books 1-3
- Mischief in Dog Town - Books 4-7
- Mischief in Dog Town - Books 8-10
- Mischief in Dog Town - The Complete Series

Made in the USA
Coppell, TX
29 July 2024

35310927R00125